A Weird Fiction Tale II:

METROPOLITAN MEXPLOITATION

A Weird Fiction Tale II:

METROPOLITAN MEXPLOITATION

JCC Chavez, Jr.

CHAPTER 1

GOOD MORNING CUCKOO MEADOWS

From radio broadcast to extensive television coverage, the entire soundscape of the great metropolis, Cuckoo Meadows, is engulfed in chatter surrounding the "Masked Philanthropist," a man whose enigmatic allure is solely rivaled by his jazzy personality.

Various tabloid magazine publications and celebrity elites poise him to be the next man of the century. Beloved by the common populace, envied by the dregs of society, no camera lens is blind to his nebulous countenance, and no ear is deaf to the chime of his name. And that name is Bloodstone, the Immortal Luchador!

Out by the outskirts of the metropolis just

off the railroad tracks that divide the Dirty Southsville borough from the rest of the city, lies a humble little establishment christened Alaska's Roshambo Café. It is here we find our lovely heroine with the name of Rubí Aquila Sierra. She is a driven and intelligent young lady with medium-length jet black hair, olive skin, and tender auburn eyes that purely examine the fragilities of one's soul.

Rubí, or Miss Sierra as her future employer will come to call her, hails from a small, reclusive town nestled deep in the northern mountains, far away from the prying eyes of the larger world. And for most of her tender years of blissful reclusiveness, Miss Sierra spent her time at the town library, face pasted flat inside the crisp pages of every bloated book at her disposal. The library's mounds of books allocated her the knowledge and experiences of more worldlier individuals than herself, and weaved written canvases that helped broaden the barrier of her fishbowl world. But it is only now, at the ripen age of nineteen, that Miss Sierra will finally learn to live beyond the scope of the scrawled page.

Against her parents' wishes, more so her father's than her absent mother's, Miss Sierra moved to Cuckoo Meadows to pursue a career in business administration with Bloodstone Enterprises. After three grueling months of living in a sardine-can studio apartment, tolerating the company of often arguing neighbors and unwanted visiting roaches, and surviving on mediocre meals of breadcrumbs, with the occasional sips of water, she has finally secured an entry-level job with the conglomerate giant. Unfortunately, the position she has applied for is shrouded in mystery. It is something of an odd practice, so she thinks to herself, to be hired for an undisclosed position and, more so, told to meet her direct supervisor at a diner out by one of Cuckoo Meadows' less illustrious boroughs.

Maybe this is some sort of a prank, an office ritual to welcome me into the company—Miss Sierra muses to herself. *I shouldn't be surprised by this oddity of a practice. I mean, come on, the company is run by the Masked Philanthropist, Bloodstone. Guy's a curious case all to himself as it is. Oops, there I go again, muttering to myself. Curse these shaky nerves of mine.*

The windy outdoor air carries the promise of a forthcoming winter, and Miss Sierra shivers in her arms. She is nervous. She looks to her wristwatch—the old watch's ticking worries her further. It is a quarter past ten of the morning, and her supervisor is running fashionably late.

She loosens her pink scarf and waves to the waitress. Miss Sierra then orders herself a hot chocolate. The service is quick. In under three minutes, she already sips on the freshly brewed, warm drink. With her contact still absent from sight, she decides to distract her nerves and takes in the morning televised gossip while it continues to cover Bloodstone's tallying acclamations after his extensive contributions to the world.

The channel is set to K-JCM TV, and anchors Toby and Robbie share the screen. Toby, a caramel-toned, thin man with smoky grey hair, is the first to speak.

TOBY

An exceptionally beautiful and chilly morning to you, Cuckoo Meadows. I hope you all remembered to wear your winter fashionables this morning as winter's frosty kiss is but a few winks of the sun away. Wouldn't you agree, Robbie?

News anchor Robbie is a fiery redhead with a smoky voice and blue eyes. She is often showcased in many pop magazines due to her charm, womanly sexuality, and pragmatic intellect. Such traits make her the perfect icon of female empowerment and the unattainable desire for a world rife with boys and scarce of respectable men.

ROBBIE

It is Toby, but the city burns hot with pride over the continuing achievements of its favorite son. That's right, folks, once again, for the sixteenth consecutive week, the Masked Philanthropist-slash-Billionaire-slash-Corporate mogul, Bloodstone is making headlines. I tell you, Toby, this man is a rolling ball of snow who's on a continuous roll towards an upward slope of universal adulation.

TOBY

Indeed, he is Robbie. For our viewers just tuning in, Robbie and I continue with our coverage of Bloodstone Enterprises' recent launch of the SETH Redemptive Foundation. A charitable foundation that promises to further enhance healthcare, reduce poverty, and expand education worldwide, and it is the brainchild of the ever charismatic and often controversial figurehead of the company. I find this to be a most noble cause, yet I am a tad more conservative about the name, a name which has sparked much controversy within the community.

ROBBIE

Controversial seems a tad too conservative, yet accurate enough, Toby. For our viewers too young to remember, the foundation's namesake is derived from none other than the legendary android leader and first scion, SETH, whose very name and reformat cycle are inextricably linked with outbreaks of rebellion and war such as Genesis' bloody Great Schism which first engulfed the mutant nation in war for near half a century seventy years ago today. Furthermore, the foundation's launch coupled with the company's recent financial backing of the Astro Punk Program has led many political leaders and scholars the world over to interpret Bloodstone's actions as an attempt to mend the fraught and strained relationship between the android republic of Exodus and the rest of the human-centric world.

TOBY

Quite right, Robbie. It seems our boy has quite the rugged road ahead of him. In another matter, Bloodstone's generosity knows no bounds as he continues giving back to his community. The master of fantastical bonfire tales has recently donated a quarter-million dollars to the Saint Augustine Rose de la Croix Orphanage. A most welcomed and needed contribution, as the orphanage was slated for closure by this year's end due to lack of funding. The massive check was accepted with utmost glee by the orphanage's headmaster, Deacon Giacomo Fulci.

ROBBIE

Even more reason for the public to adore the Masked Philanthropist, Toby. He is a man of the people for the people, a beacon of inspiration, an advocate of peace and equality, and without a doubt, our man of the century. And to further expand on the

SETH Redemptive Foundation subject, I would like to remind our viewers that the foundation is a joint venture with Corvus Technologies and is slated to be managed directly by Corvus' President and heir, Sir Maximus Aurelius Gold, who earlier this week held a public press conference with a Bloodstone Enterprises representative to publicly outline the first proposed set of programs which will provide vast financial and technological support to various outsourced nonprofit organizations. The programs aim to develop progressive solutions that will, in turn, halt further deforestation of the Amazon. In addition to these proposed programs, the foundation will continue to spearhead projects that will diversify the reintegration of the android populace into suburbs nationwide. This is no doubt another of Bloodstone's attempts to moderate the peaceful mending of human-android relations. I tell you, Toby, even with the stability of the world perched atop his broad shoulders, there is simply no stopping this man.

TOBY

He is a man without limitations or equal Robbie. Now, there was something you said back there that has got my ears itching and my curiosity twitching, Robbie.

ROBBIE

Really? Pray tell Toby, don't go all shy on me now. Go ahead and speak your mind.

TOBY

A week ago, just before the foundation's launch, I thought the press conference was supposed to be moderated by both Sir Maximus Gold and Bloodstone himself. Yet, the Masked Philanthropist failed to make an appearance at the conference. Instead, the crowded room, which included yours truly, had to settle conversing with a rather meek and uncharismatic intern. The whole thing seemed a bit uncharacteristic of Bloodstone, who has never been one to shy away from any press conference due to harsh criticism from hecklers. My question then is, why did he fail to make an appearance?

ROBBIE

I'm glad you finally asked that question, Toby, and let me put your doubts to rest. His absence was not an intentional snub aimed at the press. You see, not everything is golden in our beloved Bloodstone's realm. Though the news was not made public knowledge immediately, we had finally received confirmation from Bloodstone Enterprises' representatives about a break-in that occurred at Bloodstone's luxury penthouse a few minutes before the press conference was to take place. As of now, only one unidentified object was reported stolen from his private vault—a most prized treasure. No further details have been released, nor has any official investigation on the theft been opened with the Cuckoo Meadows Police Department. Apparently, Bloodstone has decided to personally take care of the matter.

TOBY

Personally, you say. That's quite an intriguing revelation, Robbie. It's not often you hear about a corporate mogul getting his hands dirty with such petty matters. What do you suppose was stolen from his vault, and why would Bloodstone decide to handle the situation personally? Wouldn't it be wiser to let the proper authorities take care of the whole situation?

ROBBIE

These are all particularly good questions, Toby. Though we know of Bloodstone the C.E.O., Bloodstone the Philanthropist, and Bloodstone the Storyteller, none of us truly knows about Bloodstone the MAN. I have had the pleasure to converse with him in the past and can say the following with conviction. He is the epitome of gentlemanly conduct and a generous, fun-loving human being. Rest assured, though he is not of fragile pride, he is not someone to be trifled with. For behind the blanket of fine suits and silk shirts lies a chiseled body of beastly masculinity

*and Greek perfection. I pray whomever
the thieves responsible for such tomfool-
ery are, are wise to whom they have just
disrespected.*

TOBY

*My, oh my, that is quite a warning—
nay, threat—right there, Robbie. Well,
that sure clarifies everything, especially
Bloodstone's recent absence from public
appearances as of late. Mr. Bloodstone,
wherever you might find yourself right
now, know that myself, Robbie and the
entire K-JCM TV family wish you the
best of luck in your quest, and we pray
for your safe return. Alright, folks, now
onto sports and weather.*

Another fifteen minutes have passed, and
there is still no sight of her contact. To make
up for lost time, Miss Sierra then decides to
go ahead and order herself a small dish of two
scrambled eggs with a side of bacon and toast,
accompanied with a cup of prime roast coffee.
The meal is adequate and enough to appease
her gnarling hunger. It is the only thing she can
scrim with her scarce budget. As she timidly

nibbles on her meal, Miss Sierra wonders if the recent theft might have anything to do with her contact's tardiness. She calls back to the day of her interview, which took place three days after the theft. The ambiance at Bloodstone Enterprises' corporate building gave no signs of pandemonium nor worry over their missing President and C.E.O. Then again, the corporate culture is just as odd as its lively founder.

Just as Miss Sierra finishes the last few sips of her coffee, the plum waitress at her beck and call quickly refills her cup with a fresh serving. The service at Alaska's Roshambo Café is quite exquisite.

"Excuse me, miss?" Miss Sierra asks shyly to the wrinkly, plum waitress. "May I bother you with the time?"

Miss Sierra quickly tucks her wristwatch under her jacket's sleeve before the waitress notices it. Although she already knows the time, impatience makes her mistrust its punctuality. Not to mention her seizure-like nerves easily toy with her delicate confidence. No one can blame her, though. Miss Sierra is but a bird learning to fly in the gale of a thunderstorm. She is the first of her family, after her mother that is, to venture out beyond the borders of their small, confined world and into the greater world in perpetuity. Expectations are high, to say the least, from within and without.

"What's that, sweetie? Oh, the time." The waitress, with the name badge that reads Betsy, looks to her own wristwatch. Squinting through her rectangular specs, she replies. "It's, uh, twenty till eleven of the a.m. Everything alright, hon? Beau is running a tad late, I wager."

"What?" Miss Sierra is taken quite aback. Betsy's passive, infantile remark makes her think she's being teased, quite mistakenly. "No, um, no. I'm not waiting for any boy. I'm expecting a business contact."

"Business contact?" Betsy, the waitress, snorts incredulously. "What sort of a business contact would have a pretty flower such as yourself meet them in a dump like this? Oh honey, don't tell me he's your pimp. You're far too pretty and fresh for that sort of a livelihood."

"Dear Lord! No ma'am. I'm waiting on a representative from Bloodstone Enterprises." Miss Sierra quickly fires back to the cloddish Betsy. "I've recently been hired with the company and was told to meet my supervisor here at ten. But it's getting close to eleven now, and I was wondering if there might have been any calls or—a pimp? Really?"

"Ho-ho-ho, there, there, sweetie. No need to be prudish about such an adulterated remark." Betsy responds with amusement. "Pay no mind to my blunt rudeness, dearie. I've lived in this fair city since I was a wee tot. Guess the environment has made me rather blunt and a stranger to civil manners. Say, you ain't from around these parts, are you? I can read that much about you. Where you hail from, hon?"

"I'm from up north, from a small town. There's no point in telling you the town's name. I'm sure you've never heard of it anyway." Miss Sierra answers shyly. Though she has been in the city for a good, few months already, she is yet to make any sort of friends or even casual acquaintances. It isn't for lack of trying, though. She simply prefers the comfort of her books. It is the only way she has ever known to socialize with others, through the stories they've imprinted over dusty, stitch-bound reams of paper.

"Up north, you say. Beyond the mountains, behind a shroud of snow and far away from the rest of us jaded city folk, I wager." Betsy sits across from Miss Sierra. She finds herself enjoying the small chitchat with the young lady and decides to take a short break from a long morning of serving tables. "I can tell, I can tell. Your eyes give it away, sweetie. Take no offense to what I'm about to say, but your eyes gleam with the ignorance of innocence, and your skin is far too smooth. It lacks the dirt and grit of a brazened city dweller."

"No offense taken . . . I think." Miss Sierra finds herself unoffended with Betsy's observations. Though the waitress speaks boldly, she speaks accurately, no less. She awkwardly smiles back at Betsy. "I'm sorry, not to change the subject, but have there been any calls for me?"

"Phone calls? Here? From whom love?" Betsy asks with uninterest. She absently pokes Miss Sierra's leftovers and sips coffee from her cup. Betsy continues, blind to Miss Sierra's puzzlement over her level of uninvited comfort. "No, there haven't been any phone calls here, hon. I'm sorry, my mind's been somewhat foggy lately. Who are you waiting for again?"

"Are you serious? I just mentioned it a minute ago. You know what, never—" Miss Sierra sighs. She rubs her eyes in frustration before continuing. "Bloodstone Enterprises.

I've been waiting for a rep from Bloodstone Enterprises, who's almost forty-five minutes late. Well, now he or she is. I need to know if there have been any calls for me here from the company."

"Bloodstone Enterprises? Oh, that's right." Betsy said enthusiastically, snapping her fingers. "Congratulations on your hiring, by the way. Say, why don't I get you a celebratory pastry over here. On the house, of course. Oi, Buck! Bring us a Chocolate Crème Bun over here for this lovely young lady! She got a gig at Bloodstone Enterprises, and we gotta celebrate it!"

"Huh? What now, for who now?" Buck the cook hollers back, confused from behind the kitchen counter. "No more freebies Betsy. Yesterday alone, you gave out over ten pity pastry goodies for birthdays, wedding anniversaries, and other whatnots, for fuck's sake. No more, you hear me?! You keep flaunting about freebies, and we'll be out of business by week's end, mark my words!"

"Heartless swine of a penny pincher! Pardon me for caring a shit's ass about others' blessings and joys!" Betsy barks to Buck before smiling warmly back to Miss Sierra. "Sorry love, no special bun after all. Cook is a real shit tart about it!"—she yells back to Buck.

"Um . . . that's quite alright." Miss Sierra said, quite embarrassed from the sudden outburst of snide remarks between the cook and waitress. The glances and giggles from the other patrons only add to her anxiety and discomfort. "I wasn't in the mood for any pastries, either way. Now, um, please, have there been any calls for me?"

Betsy twists her lips, confused with the repeated question. Much to Miss Sierra's continued ire. She begins to question if Betsy is possibly a bit senile.

"Hm? Oh, dearie me, went off the rails again, didn't I?" Betsy chortles. "Sorry, angel pie, old age tends to distract the mind. One minute I'm sharp as a whistle. The next minute, I'm chasing imaginary butterflies down a dank alley. Ha-ha. Oi, so you said Bloodstone Enterprises. Funny you should say that. We get a lad from the company who usually frequents the diner every morning. Come to think about it. He's unusually late today. Very strange. Thing is the lad happens to be—"

A loud boom suddenly stuns both women silent. The outside winds burst through the diner's doors in a chilled rush. A shaggy beggar has entered the diner in the most dramatic of ways. With a powerful swing of the door, the beggar announces his arrival to the dining patrons. The clattering of dining tools stills and goes silent after a wave of surprised gasps.

Through long, thin strands of seaweed-like hairs, the beggar glares at the small crowd with bloodshot eyes that pulse with madness and gleam with fearsome delusions of chaos and anarchy. The beggar's clothes are torn down to the seams. He bears a long, booger-green trench coat spritzed with stains of questionable origin. And his shoes barely conceal the callus toes ill with fungus which peek out from the holes gnawed out through the soles by the rasp of time.

The beggar scratches the wild, frizzy beard gnarled around his face. He then takes in a whiff of the diner's ambiance. An expression of utter disgust scrunches up his greasy, dirty face inward. Miss Sierra surveys the confused, worried faces of the other patrons. Some cover their mouths to hold back the streams of vomit grating their throats. Though she is not equally rude, Miss Sierra does not blame them. The beggar's unnatural musk reeks of shit, piss, and

God knows what other foul stenches. A rotting corpse would let off a far more pleasant fragrance. The smell becomes too unbearable, and Miss Sierra soon joins the other patrons in their crude salute. She cups her mouth and smacks her lips with distaste. The beggar's rotting smell has defiled the sanctity of her taste buds.

"All right, pal." Buck approaches the smelly beggar with a spatula clutch on the right hand. "Not to offend you or anything of the sort, but the rules here are simple and sacred like the word of the Lord. No shoes. No shirt. No bath. No service. So, I'm gonna have to ask you politely to turn tail and haul your stinky ass outta my diner—geez Louise, heavens man. The fuck . . .? What in the many hells have you been doing? Smells like you've been marinating in manure under the hot sun. Ugh, I was mistaken. Manure don't reek as bad."

"Buck! Now that is being too forward with him, you, insensitive clod." Betsy rushes up to the beggar. She shoves Buck to the side and attempts to appease the beggar's tempered psyche with warm hospitality. "Pardon him, dearie. He must have dropped his brains in the fryer again. Say, why don't we prep you a nice breakfast sandwich to go, and we can just put this whole rudeness behind—"

WHAM!

Without warning or provocation, the beggar pulls out a concealed shotgun and slams Betsy right across the jaw with the barrel. The bludgeon force knocks the plum waitress clear across the floor with a stream of blood trailing right behind her.

"Betsy!" Buck wails in shock.

"What . . .? What the hell's your problem?! You, crazy, son of a bitch! I was only showing you kindness. Showing you decency and respect!" Betsy screams, horrified. She spews out bubbles of blood and spits out loosened teeth.

"Shut your trap, you fat cow!" The beggar commands with a surly growl. He cocks the shotgun and fires a warning shot up at the ceiling. Wails of fear and horror pierce the patrons' initial gasps. Then, the mad beggar begins to ramble his sermon with a drool. "All right! You, drooling, mindless, castrated lumps of organic waste, I'm here to peel away the oniony layers of ignorance you've feasted upon your entire worthless lives. With every layer peeled, I shall reveal the one, absolute truth, and it'll singe thy eyes and produce tears of cruel revelation!"

"Shut your trap, you cum shot reject!" Buck slaps the raving beggar across the face with his spatula. His anger is fueled by what the maniac has done to poor, old Betsy. "That there was for me dear old friend Betsy. Fat cow she may be, but no one, especially a cretinous piss stain like you, lays a heavy hand on her delicate features. And no one goes popping holes on my fine establishment without getting an earful from yours truly. Now take your crazy, little sermon outta here and keep it out with the rest of them loon patrol nuts 'fore I scrape your pungent carcass off my grill with this here spatula!"

Hailing from a small, reclusive town, where the biggest squabbles between neighbors are over the most inconsequential of material possessions, Miss Sierra is unfamiliar with such barbaric theatrics and is dumbstruck with panic and awe. Though flabbergasted, her eyes glow with sincere admiration over the cook's bravery. Despite Buck's earlier crude attitude towards Betsy, his brave stance to defend her honor is a testament to their knotty love and shared respect for one another. Behind her beguiled trance, Miss Sierra cheers the cook's bravado.

Her entire body shakes with uneasiness, but not out of fear. On the contrary, the virgin maiden fights the impulsion to act and join in the fray to ward off the raving lunatic. But such noble intentions fall under the yoke of her father's stern voice. On the day she left for Cuckoo Meadows, Miss Sierra's father urged her to keep to herself and avoid all unpleasant and dangerous situations.

For the moment, she obeys her father's distant pleas and observes with defiance.

The beggar wipes off the small stream of blood trickling down his nose. He caresses the red fluid between his right index finger and thumb, amused by it. He sneers back to the unsuspecting cook, Buck, and the beggar bludgeons him with his forehead. The cook's nose pops in a fresh burst of blood.

Buck falls over on his back. He yowls and cradles his freshly tenderized nose. The blood continues to flood out. He screams, "Argh! Damn crazy . . . ass . . . son of a whore, gone busted up my nose!"

"Buck! You damn, brave stubborn buffoon!" Betsy yelps out in horror.

"Shut up! All of you! Just shut your yammering arses!" The beggar scowls at the top of his lungs, clawing his scalp. And everyone obeys. He then points the shotgun's barrel directly at Buck's crotch and growls to the whimpering cook with gnashing rotten, blackened teeth. "See what happens when you try to silence the voice of truth, you shit munching maggot. It fights back! Yeah, baby! It fights back with bludgeoning scalps and crackling knuckles, baby! Har-har-har!"

The beggar guffaws maniacally. The patrons do nothing except watch in petrified horror.

CHAPTER 2

BATHED IN MILK

Raving madly like a bloodthirsty hyena, the beggar's insanity pins Alaska's Roshambo Café's small flock of patrons under fear's thumb. Everyone takes a cowardly posture and does nothing to fight back, their joints and wills are frozen stiff with the natural impulse to preserve oneself. Everyone, except for Miss Sierra. She stands defiant and rises from her seat to carefully evaluate her next move.

"Brothers! Sisters! Lend me thy deaf ears!" The beggar continues to force down his unwelcomed sermon upon the people. "We are but simple, stupid sheep who flock blindly to the command of our shepherds, who are shameless wolves without alternative guise. We continue to mindlessly nibble on the green prairie of mediocrity. Waken your taste buds, my fellow sheep, and you will see that we do not dine on grass, rather shit. That's right, shit, baby! Har-har-har!"

Miss Sierra tilts on the edge of her toes. She has had quite enough of the stark raving lunatic and casually begins to tiptoe towards the counter, closer to the beggar. *If father could only see me right now*, she thinks to herself. *Surely, he'd disapprove. What did he say to me that one day, some odd years ago, when the bounty killers purged our little town of a great evil?— Oh yeah. We are but two sides of the same coin. Bravery is merely another measure of idiocy. Well, father, sorry to disappoint you, but your little girl is equally brilliant as she is brave and stupid.*

The beggar pauses but for a moment. He snorts like a filthy swine and blows his bloodied nose. He snickers mischievously then plucks and flings a bloodied booger straight at Buck. The cook flinches in fear and quivers like a frightened, freshly spanked child. Poor Buck, the bravado he barked up earlier has effectively been quashed with the blunt of madness.

"Now, where was I?" The beggar asks, sincerely lost. The nose pick has easily waylaid his tract of thoughts. He churns an irate growl that summons pathetic whimpers from the flock of mindless sheep. "Anyone know where I left off?!—rude! The lot of you, for not paying me proper attention! Maybe a healthy dose of lead will teach y'all proper decorum. You, spineless sheep!"

The shotgun is cocked, and the people start to scatter away to all corners of the diner like roaches on the flicker of the light. Just then, Miss Sierra steps in without a wink of fear in her eyes. Her voice is steady and confident.

"Stop!" She screams. Their eyes lock. Miss Sierra looks straight into the beggar's shaky, vein throbbing mad eyes. She is utterly unamused with the smelly man's shallow threats and speaks to him with reserved defiance. "We are shit munching sheep. That's what you were saying last. So please, lower the shotgun and do go on with your . . . enlightening lecture."

Such affected words leave a bad taste in her mouth. Miss Sierra is unaccustomed to fibbing, much less curbing her disdain towards heinous creatures like the beggar. But the situation demands she bite her tongue and swallow down her often-opinionated words.

The beggar purses his lips, tilts his head slightly crabwise. He muses for a second and addresses Miss Sierra politely with a far tamer and somewhat sane tune. "That's quite right. Shit eating sheep 'twas. Why, thank you, miss." He then shifts back to his old insane self in a blink of an eye, and the beggar resumes with his senseless rhetoric. "Shit, baby! That's what your bureaucratic wolves are feeding us. Shit seasoned with deceptive magnanimity, and what do we do?! We eagerly gather around the trough—like pigs to the slaughter and gorge down the shit like filth grubbing maggots! People open your peepers, and you will see that we are not sheep at all! We are a composite monstrosity of sheep, swine, and maggot! A vile rib-tickler of mythological proportions! Wee Piglet Sheep-Maggots that is what we are! Har-har-har!"

Miss Sierra gently slips on her kiddie gloves and attempts to humor the beggar's drooling madness. "Of course, it all makes sense. How did we never see the truth before? You are our hero, a brave warrior of truth who speaks up against the sinister oppressors who continue to enslave us honest folk with lies and deception. Such noble efforts merit universal praise."

"Hon, what are you doing?" Betsy whispers to her, spitting out another tooth.

"Trying to save our skins, Betsy. Now hush

and let me handle the situation." Miss Sierra whispers back to the shaken waitress before turning back to the beggar. "Oh, brave warrior of the truth, wouldn't it be nice if you could share your wisdom with the rest of the world? To deprive it of such revolutionary philosophical teachings is but a crime, if not staggering, um, idiocy."

"Huh?" The beggar scratches his bushy beard, truly enamored with Miss Sierra's words. The thought of his gospel being heard nationwide is intoxicating to his psychosis-inebriated brain. "Yes, yes, yeah, baby! I speak the voice of truth, and it cannot be limited to the ears of these pitiful maggots. The one, universal truth is like a genital infection. It cannot be selfishly squandered. No, it must be shared. That is the one, universal truth. Yeah, baby!—but, uh, but, but how do we do that?"

The beggar pouts like a pathetic stray dog and turns to Miss Sierra for guidance with expectant eyes. The clever girl snails her hands upward toward the ceiling, both palms opened. Miss Sierra wants to dilute any ideas of rebellion or deceit on her part, as not to provoke an angry outburst from the unstable beggar. She points to her jacket's left pocket with a dipping finger.

Miss Sierra explains her every action thereafter to the unhinged beggar, who narrows his slits and eagerly hovers the shotgun's barrel over her bosom. "Let me pull out my cellphone, and with a single call, I can have every single media outlet come out here within minutes. That way, the rest of this underserving nation will get the privilege of rejoicing in your wizened words, oh exalted one."

The beggar gives her a crooked smile and drools hungrily like a rabid dog. He reaches into his pants and starts rubbing his cock. The idea itself excites him in more ways than Miss Sierra cares to know.

"Oh, baby . . . yeah. Me likey that very much. Talk to me, girl! Thought of it all throbs my cock with demonic hunger, baby!" The beggar pants and licks his lips with licentious hunger, much to Miss Sierra's discomfort. "Get that Robbie babe down here too. Not that skunk furred Toby, though! Can't stand the whiff of his musk. Reeks of other men's junk and sweat. Yuck!"

"As you wish, warrior of truth." Miss Sierra replies with as much feigned sincerity she can muster. She stills her shaky hands for two strenuous minutes, enough time to dial the sole number at her disposal—her sole gamble. Not a single drop of sweat trickles down her face, not even when doubt caresses her neck.

Oh, now you've done it, girl. How the hell are you going to pull it all off? Get the entire media down here?! Grr . . . why couldn't you listen to papá for once?! She chides herself and holds the phone close to her ears, unsure if the ringing will ever cease. *Bravery and idiocy are but two sides of the same coin. Well, the coin has been tossed, papá. I do pray it lands upright instead of flat.*

⸻ ⸻

Her wristwatch reads eleven a.m. Miss Sierra sighs with a breath of optimism and smiles. Outside the diner, she snatches sight of a quickly amassing crowd, a mix of gossipy onlookers, news reporters—including the fiery redhead Robbie—and a squad of half a dozen surly police officers.

Miss Sierra makes a mental note to personally thank Bloodstone Enterprises' shrewd secretary. Still unfamiliar to the colorful inhabitants who inhabit the grandiose city of

Cuckoo Meadows, Miss Sierra's contact list is scarce and dry of names and digits. The only number available to her, aside from her father's, is the company's senior secretary. Fortune was kind to her. The secretary, whose name is Yasmine, handled her dire situation with compassion and urgency. The assemblage outside Alaska's Roshambo Café conveys to Miss Sierra that Yasmine used Bloodstone Enterprises' immeasurable clout to contact Cuckoo Meadows' illustrious news outlets and the city's police commissioner and alerted them to the hostage situation taking place at the beleaguered diner.

Within five minutes, the tatty venue was sprawling with intrigue and curious individuals.

A yellow riot tape is spread across and tied to orange cones, and a delicate barrier is created to temper the advancing crowds of wide-eyed spectators.

"All right, keep all of them nosy bystanders at bay, boys!" Hollers the officer in charge. A coarse and crude man, Officer Harrigan is not the most sociable of men. His utter disdain for other human beings is baffling, as he is a devout practitioner of absolute law and order and a proud defender of public civil order. He chomps on a block of tobacco and sprays out brown spittle while he rehearses the situation to his men. "Seems we got us a mad dog in there, lads. He's been drooling church-like nonsense to a pack of timid bunnies. To top it off, the mad dog has got himself a boom-stick as well. So, let us handle the situation with a delicate hand when it comes down to negotiations. We'll blindside the mad dog with lies and play the part of a humbled fool. Now let's go save all of them bunnies without a scratch and slam the sick fuck behind bars."

The clamoring crowds begin to scratch at Officer Harrigan's nerves, even more so when he notices a tall man gently plowing through the crowds with his purring motorcycle. The mysterious man sports a pair of black biker boots, blue jeans with a short-length chain that jingles at his right side, a black leather jacket, and keeps his face concealed behind the helmet's darkened visor.

"That just tears it!" Officer Harrigan storms towards the man, ready to impose his authority with rawness and impunity. "Hey! What the fuck are you thinking, riding a bike into the crowd like that?! What, are you blind, stupid, or something? This here is a crime scene, pal, so haul that bike back to the curb and wait for us to do our job properly."

"My apologies for the rudeness constable, but such rudeness is very much necessitated, if not justified." The man shuts off the motorcycle's engine and steps off the seat. The man proves to be much taller and easily towers over Officer Harrigan. He addresses the burly officer with a well-mannered tone despite his condescending attitude. "For you must understand, I am rather late for a most important meeting in this fine establishment here. And I do not wish to keep a particular young lady waiting much longer."

The man removes his helmet and reveals not a face but a masked visage. The mask is mainly solid white, with thick-black trims outlining the openings of the eyes, nose, and mouth. And a swirling, black conch shell is stenciled just above the brow area of the mask. A choir of surprised gasps follows the surprising revelation.

Officer Harrigan sneers at the man and bellows angrily. "Aw, hell no. Not you. Not now, of all times. Who the fuck called you out here this time?!"

Finally, after a week of absence from public appearances and over an hour late for his appointment with Miss Sierra, the one and only—the Masked Philanthropist himself—Bloodstone has finally arrived.

"I don't give a naked mole's ass about who you are within the community, Bloodstone." Officer Harrigan barks to an indifferent Bloodstone. He taps him rudely on the chest unafraid that even Bloodstone's shadow dwarfs him. "I'm the sheriff in this here town and the ringleader of this here circus. You may have the largest bank account in town, but that don't make you anything exceptional or an exception to our laws. You are still nothing more than a mere citizen to me. Which means I can have you arrested at the snap of my fingers if I see it fit to do so."

"Hm?" Bloodstone feigns inattentiveness, not for rudeness's sake, just sheer enjoyment. He and Officer Harrigan have a long, legendary history of headbutting. The Masked Philanthropist's reputable impulsiveness and chivalrous posture conflict with Officer Harrigan's oft-brutal methods of law enforcement. With subtle sarcasm, Bloodstone continues. "My dear constable, I am most confused by this blatant rudeness aimed at my person. I don't recall ever having stepped on your toes."

Officer Harrigan's left brow cracks with hot, webby veins. He huffs hotter steam towards Bloodstone. "Don't mock my intelligence, you two-cent gimp! Now get behind the line with the rest of the—the—where the fuck, do you think you're going?!"

Bloodstone has quickly grown bored toying with Officer Harrigan's ill-temper. He nonchalantly bypasses the yellow tape barrier and marches towards the diner. "As I had mentioned earlier, constable, I am rather late for a most important meeting. Feel free to try and arrest me if you wish. Just consider yourself forewarned; such bravery will prove most detrimental to the physical wellbeing of your men. Yourself included, of course." Midway towards Alaska's Rashambo Café, Bloodstone pauses and addresses Officer Harrigan alone. He never turns to face him. "Oh, and constable. Be thankful I did not cave in your jaw for that vulgar remark you fired back at me just now. With my considerable wealth and influence, I could've easily gotten away with it. You are forgiven . . . this time."

Officer Harrigan is left stunned and speechless for the first time in his twelve years of duty. Legitimate fear has swiftly humbled him.

Scorned, he can only gawk and watch Blood-stone continue his defiant march towards the diner in utter silence.

The doorbell dings when Bloodstone walks in, and all eyes present gaze upon him.

Miss Sierra is in immediate awe of Bloodstone's mere presence. The Masked Philanthropist looks to both Betsy and Buck, visibly disturbed with their bloodied faces. Then, to Miss Sierra's sincere surprise, he winks at her like a mischievous child on the ready to unleash some sort of mischief. Then, with stern seriousness, Bloodstone locks eyes with the mad beggar.

"My friend," Bloodstone speaks to the beggar with a cold breath, "would you mind sharing your name with me?"

"Name?" The beggar asks with a twisted snarl. "I got no name. Names are nothing more than spectral shackles used by the establish-ment to keep us under a leash, forever enslaved to a decadent society's sick and perverse nym-phomaniac desires till our last, dying breath. Filthy, dirty, and loathsome whores, that's what we are! That's the one, universal truth! Can't you see it?!"

It is most impressive, not the beggar's

incoherent drools, but Bloodstone's calm demeanor. The once frightened hostages have now become awestruck spectators. They all understand the one truth the beggar is too blind to see—the situation is well within Bloodstone's absolute control. He has already won the battle.

"My dear, delusional maniac, I've suckled on the nectar of everlasting life for nigh three centuries now and have swatted pitiful, child-ish demonic lords on a tantrum as if they were nothing more than bothersome flies. Knowledge of unto which depths the mythical paradise of Tlalocan has hidden itself onto is mine alone to know. I was there to groom the newborn intelligence on the cruelties of life. And I know with absolute confidence that the one, universal truth is ever-evolving and forever elusive as memory itself. And you, my friend, know nothing."

"Har-har-har! You're crazier than I am and plain stupid." The beggar overlooks Blood-stone's subtle threat. His eyes bulge madly, and he drills a finger into his right ear to scrape for ear wax. An extremely dangerous mistake. "I'm the face of the new world to come, and your big words were, like, totally disrespectful towards me, yeah?"

"Hmph, I've met your kind before, and no matter how much times have changed, you always remain the same, stupid and prone to a bruising. You're nothing more than common trash, my friend. An inconvenient chewed-up piece of gum stuck on the soles of my boots. Ergo, I shall baptize you with a common name—Joe sounds appropriate enough." Bloodstone then takes notice of the beggar's shotgun and recants his remark. "Better yet, Shotgun Joe."

"Shotgun . . . Joe? Har-har-har!" The newly christened Shotgun Joe bellows with satisfaction. "I like it! Love it, baby!"

"I'm glad you love it." Bloodstone casually reaches inside his jacket's inner pocket and pulls out a pen, checkbook, and a single bronze penny. He works to scribble on the check and addresses Shotgun Joe. "One must have a name, after all. How else do you ever expect to cash this $2999.99 check?"

What the hell? This guy bludgeons two decent folks and holds us hostage at gunpoint and gets a meaty check for it. Hell no, this is nonsense. Miss Sierra thinks to herself in disbelief. She is somewhat bashful for feeling a tad envious of Shotgun Joe. But she will come to realize the error of her premature judgment. The day is yet young, and Miss Sierra has yet much to learn about the Masked Philanthropist's many eccentricities.

"Check?" Shotgun Joe shares Miss Sierra's sourness towards Bloodstone's perplexing gesture. "I've no need for your moneys, you polished turd! You can't silence the truth with the vile green poison of society!"

"Oh no, no, no, my dear Shotgun Joe." Bloodstone chuckles, waving a finger. "I dare not buy out your, um, integrity. No, no, you will soon find out the moneys will come in handy when you find yourself broken and bathing in milk."

"Huh?" Shotgun Joe grunts.

Bloodstone pinches the penny between his fingers, holds it up, and then flips and catches it midair. He explains to the confused Shotgun Joe. "And this here penny shall bring the grand total to an even three-grand, my bath soap-challenged friend. Now, I know what you are thinking. Why bother with a measly penny? Allow me to educate you on the why my friend. Do not be so quick to dismiss a penny like everyone else, for a penny is symbolic in nature. It tethers between wealth and poverty. A penny can easily be the first of many fortunes to come or the last desperate crumb of broken avarice."

Shotgun Joe scratches his shaggy beard. His eyes grow heavy with thought. He is desperate to comprehend Bloodstone's life lesson. "Milk? Pennies?—What the fuck are you rambling about? This some sort of a bad joke?"

"My dear Shotgun Joe . . . life is but a cruel jokester . . ." Bloodstone launches the penny straight at Shotgun Joe with a flick of the finger and without warning. The tiny metal coin pierces through the air like a bullet fired from a revolver and collides with the madman's left eye. The eye bursts in a loud splash of blood, and is left totally blind.

"Argh! My eye! You've blinded me! You son of a—" Shotgun Joe's agonized wails are cut short. The blood made it difficult for him to have noticed Bloodstone defy his muscular physique and dash in a blur right in front of him. He only whimpers for a mere second. "N—No, this . . . this isn't fair . . ."

". . . and we are but the punchline to its cruel jokes," Bloodstone concludes with a glint of cold sarcasm, right before he smacks Shotgun Joe with a locomotive fueled downward arching punch to the face.

The force of Bloodstone's punch is cartoonishly powerful. It slams Shotgun Joe down on the floor with a boom of gravel and tile, just before he ricochets upward like a rubber ball, right through the diner's ceiling and topples several hundred feet up in the open air.

It will be few seconds before Shotgun Joe comes crashing back down again. Bloodstone takes these few precious seconds to dust his leather jacket off from debris, snap his neck and crack his knuckles. But Shotgun Joe will never hit the floor a second time. Midway down through the ceiling—through his silhouetted form—Bloodstone karate kicks him across, towards the kitchen. Shotgun Joe crashes unconscious inside a cooler housing two-gallon bottles of milk. And just like that, it is all over.

Bloodstone marches up to the comatose Shotgun Joe and throws the check at his heel while he bathes in milk. "Your check, my good man. Hospital bills do pile up, after all." Bloodstone said coolly.

It was a spectacular display of graceful brutality. Miss Sierra lays hypnotized with admiration. Bloodstone's mythical physical prowess and legendary chivalry are everything the people have said it to be.

"You must be Miss Sierra," Bloodstone looks down at her with a smile. Miss Sierra was caught up daydreaming and did not notice when the Masked Philanthropist walked up towards her. Flustered, she blushes shyly and is speechless. Bloodstone chuckles. "As you might know by now, without a doubt, I am Bloodstone, and you, my dear, are to be my new personal assistant. Pleasure to make your acquaintance."

CHAPTER 3

A FEAST FIT FOR AN IMMORTAL

"My humblest apologies Miss Sierra," Bloodstone said between bites. Apparently, he hasn't eaten in several days, and his hunger has gotten rather beastly. "I hope my tardiness has not soured our blossoming relationship. But as you might have heard by now, a few days back, there was a break-in at my skyward penthouse wherein a group of unknown miscreants stole something of great value to me. In all honesty, the theft of my most prized treasure has left me feeling somewhat . . . violated. Since that day, I've been tirelessly scouring the city, trying my best to apprehend the guilty scoundrels."

"It's okay sir, I, um, understand." Miss

Sierra said shyly and takes another tiny nibble from her bagel.

The young maiden looks on with amazement while Bloodstone continues to scarf down his hearty meal. Shortly after Shotgun Joe was carried out on a stretcher, still unconscious, and after enduring a great verbal assault from Officer Harrigan—his squad had to drag the boorish officer away mid-rant when his face turned red and on the brink of a heart attack—Bloodstone offered to take up Betsy and Buck's medical bills, plus pay for the damages he impetuously caused to their diner. The Masked Philanthropist, true to his generous nature, expected nothing in return from the pair. Not even their praises, except, perhaps, for a warm meal from Buck the cook.

It was quite the feast too.

Bloodstone ordered four dishes of triple-stacked blueberry pancakes, three dozen eggs with twenty strips of crunchy bacon on the side, along with three slices of ham and two slices of wheat toast—no hash browns, he cares not for any type of potato. Next came a pint of orange juice and a cup of coffee to help rinse everything down. Finally, the feast fit for an immortal is topped off with a single slice of tangerine.

Miss Sierra was encouraged to order something for herself. Only after Bloodstone's tireless insisting did she finally settle for a bagel spread thinly with cream cheese.

"Please, Miss Sierra, let us dispense with this sir rubbish. Freely address me by name, Bloodstone, and nothing more. We are to be friends, after all." Bloodstone said purely to Miss Sierra. He munches on the last few morsels of his bacon and pats his hardened gut contently.

"I'm sorry . . . but I don't think I can do that, actually." Miss Sierra's stern mother, whom she hardly spoke of or spoke to for that matter, has educated her to always address her perceived betters by their proper titles of authority. It is a programmed mindset she earnestly tries to purge from her willful spirit. It isn't an easy task to accomplish, but at the least, she can think of an adequate compromise to this foolish dilemma. "Um . . . perhaps *Mister* Bloodstone would be more comfortable for the both of us."

Bloodstone sips his coffee, and his eyes glitter with satisfaction toward her proposition. "Splendid suggestion!" He exclaims. "Very well, *Mister* Bloodstone it is then."

"Yes, well, if you don't mind me saying so, um, Mister Bloodstone, you sort of caught me unawares back there." Miss Sierra never suspected she applied for the position of Bloodstone's personal assistant. This is truly an astonishing revelation for her.

At the time of her interview, the string of questions she was asked was odd, to say the least. Yasmine, the young senior secretary, interviewed her and asked only three questions: Do you believe a prancing unicorn would ever dance with a human-sized Ironwood Beetle under the pale blue moonlight during a midsummer night? If asked to do so, are you willing to rub honey-glazed balm, extracted from the mucus-secreting warts of the extra-dimensional, bull-sized, cannabis-smoking Mammoth Toads, on a fully nude, well-chiseled male form? And lastly, do you know how to swim?

She would have laughed at such ludicrous and hilarious questions if not for Yasmine's stiff face—Miss Sierra was aware the secretary examined her with deathlike seriousness. After a short, discomforting minute, Miss Sierra answered with a cautious yes.

"I mean, nowhere throughout the interview

was your secretary crystal about the job's nature." Miss Sierra continues. Though charmed with this wonderful opportunity bequeathed to her by blind chance, she isn't quite easily flattered with Bloodstone's legendary celebrity. He might be a behemoth of wealth and charisma to his legions of worshippers, but she merely sees him for what he is—a man. "And the string of questions asked of me, well, they were highly irregular and . . . weird. Anyway, I had much to suspect about the job as much as I had little to expect."

"Weird, you say? Hm, I suppose such inquiries do linger on the fringe of normalcy. Still, they served a good purpose—to give you a taste of the bizarre happenings you will surely encounter while on the job, my dear." Bloodstone said before suckling on his tangerine. "I assure you this is no ordinary job, and I no ordinary employer. Believe it or not, before you sits a man who's spelunked onto the deepest pits of perdition to arouse a century's war against the Lord of the Flies himself, Beelzebub. A man, whose self-imposed damnation culminated in a year-long lewd love affair with the Queen of the Vampires. Miss Sierra, you must understand this one unswallowable truth: my life lacks nothing but boredom alone. I promise you, starting today, each day will be a promise of a new and bizarre adventure for us."

"You're speaking of fairytales and escapist yarns, Mister Bloodstone. Vampires, a century's war against the hordes of hell, Tlalocan, and immortality. It's all a fantastical farce, much like what religion is considered nowadays. Next thing you'll be telling me magick is real." Miss Sierra meets Bloodstone's eyes and notes they are humorless. The Masked Philanthropist tilts his head knowingly and gives her a sly smirk. This is all so very strange to her. "You-you're joking, right?"

"You still doubt me . . . understandable. Though there may be some slight exaggerations in the tall tales I recite, Miss Sierra, 'tis all historically accurate—to the best of my recollection, anyway." Bloodstone remarks modestly. The greater world applauds his eccentricities, but to Bloodstone, the cheering voices often fall silent. For no amount of wealth can afford him an escape from the lickspittles nor freedom from the gilded cage of loneliness. Unbeknownst to Miss Sierra, Bloodstone welcomes her disbelief with joy. In her, he finds a voice rich with the skepticism he desperately longs.

"Then again," Bloodstone continues, "seeing is believing, is it not? I ask nothing of you, Miss Sierra, except that you always carry yourself with the same honesty you demonstrate now. Our journey together is yet to begin, and I advise you to keep an open mind—to expect the unexpected, for the madness of our imaginations will soon be left unbound. Therefore, I ask you, Miss Sierra, do you solemnly swear to boldly speak your voice with unbridled brutality, and will you trust that I, Bloodstone, speak not of fairytales but gospel truths?"

Miss Sierra is still a stranger to Cuckoo Meadows and to the broader world. She has constructed a vision of what the world must be, built over a foundation of the books absorbed in her youth. Now Bloodstone, the Immortal Luchador, challenges the rigidity of that very vision with his stories of pantomime hijinks and promises of a far more wondrous existence. Miss Sierra has left the comfort of her reclusive little town yearning to nibble a tiny glimpse of the greater world beyond her inland island. But never did she fathom this paradigm of lunacy, this Masked Philanthropist, would dare to offer her far more than she could ever chew.

For a pause of a heartbeat, she carefully

considers her response. Adventures the likes of which she has never dared to dream await her, and it is a seductive thought that ensnares her blossoming womanhood with unexplored pleasures. Before this moment, her life has been a tired, banal and safe existence, and she has thirsted for more glorious happenings for far too long.

"Yes . . . yes, I swear—I swear to it all." She replies. A burgeoning childlike wonder consumes her soul. Miss Sierra is excited about the unknown.

"Good!" Bloodstone exclaims enthusiastically. He pounds his fists over the table. The jubilant boom startles Betsy, who scurries behind the counter in fearful haste.

"For the love of goodness, you masked ruffian! You gone and scared me half to death. Thought it was that Shotgun Joe, back to exact his vengeance upon us all!" Betsy yells back to Bloodstone. She quivers with fear behind the counter.

"Oi Betsy, you really are daffy. You forget old Bloodstone here plucked him good. Bloke's all broken and won't be terrorizing these here parts anytime soon." Buck hollers back to Betsy with a mischievous grin. His voice is nasally, and his bandaged-up nose makes him look like a pudgy piglet.

The pair start squabbling among themselves again. Despite the diner's roughed-up condition, the ambiance has reverted to its jovial mood before Shotgun Joe's unwelcomed sermon. Bloodstone chuckles. He tugs his shirt's collar, somewhat ashamed for causing the squabbling. But there are far more important matters on his mind, and time is of the essence.

"Fantastic!" Bloodstone jumps off his seat. "Now, Miss Sierra, let us take our leave, for our first adventure awaits us. Let us trek through the dark and dangerous corners of this fair city, expose the thieving rogues and retrieve that which is rightfully mine."

"Yes, um, Mister Bloodstone . . ." Her heart pounces with the ferocity of an earthquake. Miss Sierra is eager to commence her new life of adventure. She halts short with one gnawing thing in need of closure. ". . . just one more question."

"Hm?" Bloodstone turns to her with a curious gaze.

"You're a multi-billionaire, no disrespect to

Betsy or Buck, but why ever did you want to meet me here of all places?"

"Quite simple, Miss Sierra," Bloodstone reaches into his jacket. He pulls out a cigar and silver Zippo lighter engraved with two dancing skeletons. He flickers on a tiny flame and lights up the cigar pinched between his lips. After a long drag from the cigar, Bloodstone blows out a thin cloud of smoke with the unmistakable scent of chocolate and continues. "I love their coffee here."

The pair make their way out of the diner. Before they step out the door, Bloodstone flings his motorcycle keys toward the register counter with his back turned away and, like a masterful marksman, perfectly dunks them inside the tip jar beside the cash register. "Keep the change, Buck, and happy birthday to your eldest boy. Hope he enjoys the bike."—the Masked Philanthropist yells back before the diner's door shuts behind them.

Bloodstone's generous gesture truly inspires Miss Sierra. Yet, ever curious, she ponders on the infinite boredom that may come with infinite wealth and professed eternal life. *What could the richest man in the world do with his rapidly sprouting riches if not flaunt it around carelessly?*

To him, a mere billion lost must be inconsequential as losing a penny from one's own pockets—she thinks to herself. Her newfound curiosity only continues to grow when she ponders on the priced item stolen from his vault.

Miss Sierra is quickly awash with foolishness, if not stupidity, to ever consider flirting with such baseless inquiries. Bloodstone does not seem the type of man to worry over bare appetites or petty trivialities. Perhaps it is a matter of pride, yes, that seems more plausible, Miss Sierra reasons. Then, she recalls Bloodstone's advice to expect the unexpected. It took a mere few seconds and paces outside Alaska's Roshambo Café for Miss Sierra to become overwhelmed trying to decipher the enigma that is Bloodstone's character.

She cannot stop pondering, though—*what could be so valuable to a self-proclaimed immortal, a multi-billionaire one to boot, that he'd be willing to divorce himself from his flourishing wealth and socialite lifestyle, to tiptoe through the murky boroughs of Cuckoo Meadows in search for a priceless trinket? Boroughs which are infested with vagabonds in the same league of madness, or worse, as Shotgun Joe.* It suddenly occurs to her that perhaps the most reasonable conclusion is the simplest—there is none madder than Bloodstone.

Time will eventually appease Miss Sierra's inquisitive cravings. For the moment, she can simply hope the prize merits the journey which lays ahead.

"Seeing as this is my first day on the job, Mister Bloodstone, pardon me for saying so. I can't help but find myself somewhat blind and lost." A cool breeze suddenly brushes past them. Miss Sierra hugs herself and tightens her scarf.

The crawling winter winds do not bother her much. She comes from a mountainous town where frostbite is as rampant as the flu. Her chills are rooted somewhere far more internal, with whispers of a familial voice suddenly deafening her thoughts. Miss Sierra hears the voice of her stern mother, and it disapproves of her every action. It further grips her breath in a fierce chokehold that cripples her delicate pride.

Miss Sierra and her mother certainly have their differences. Much like heaven's angels and hell's devils have theirs.

"Lost? How so?" Bloodstone asks. He then takes another drag from the cigar.

"Well, for starters, you've already been

searching for this stolen treasure of yours for about a week. Without obvious luck, I may add. And I'm certain you've scoured the entire city by now. So where do you propose we should start looking?" Again, she hears her mother's scolding. Vile, cruel things echo from ear to ear. Miss Sierra squints her eyes to silence the irritable chants with a chilled breath. "And where exactly do I fit in on this adventurous outfit of ours?"

"Luck has proven most elusive as of late, I admit. But worry not, my most inquisitive Miss Sierra, for I have finally stumbled upon a clue that will surely lead us to the heinous individuals who dared fancy themselves clever thieves. As a matter of fact, we must hurry if we are to make it to Sugar Hill Pier by one-thirty. I was able to arrange a meeting with a most valuable ally there. If anyone can steer us in the right direction, it is he." Bloodstone slings the tiny cigar stub to the curb and starts marching down the street hastily. "As for your role in this adventurous outfit of ours, my dear, understand one thing only— 'tis a more respectable role than a heroic sidekick or dignified squire. From here on out, we are equal partners, and you shall shape your role in this partnership into whatever you see it fit to be."

"Mister Bloodstone, wait!" Miss Sierra is a smidge above the five-foot mark and, like most of the populace, is easily dwarfed by the towering Bloodstone. While his steps are measured in a casual walk, she sprints eagerly behind and tries her best to keep a steady pace beside him. "It is a quarter till one, and Sugar Hill Pier is clear across town. Without your motorcycle, we will never make it there on time. I don't understand why you gave it away, to begin with, knowing you had to be across town."

"Now, now, there's no need for us to attach ourselves to material trinkets nor address the ironic hypocrisy of my logic. Besides, I can always buy another bike, and we can take the subway to Sugar Hill Pier from here."

"The—the subway . . ." Miss Sierra gulps at the mention of the subway. From day zero at Cuckoo Meadows, she has avoided using the underground subway at every turn. Something about the gaping mouth and echoing snarl of the train below always whisks her away to a horrific childhood memory of death and of a corrupting evil.

Over six years ago, her little brother had

met a gruesome, violent death deep inside the bowls of a mysterious subterranean tower. The accursed structure erupted in the western coast, a few miles past her hometown. There, within this vile womb, a dark birth almost destroyed her mountainous world. The last memory Miss Sierra has of her brother is of the butchered corpse returned to her father.

Miss Sierra is the sole surviving child of Salvatore Antonio Sierra, a respectable archeological historian, scholar, and socialite, social activist Charlotte Amelia Foix.

Well-oiled with the lucid fantasies of love and against the wisdom of their families, both married at the malleable age of twenty-five. Salvatore is a noble man ruled by his heart and of uncompromising integrity. As for Charlotte, she is a willful woman of a sharp intellect, from a prideful bloodline, and though she loved Salvatore, she was averse to forfeiting her family name for love alone. Two years after they were wed, they welcomed their first child into their union and named her Rubí Aquila Sierra. Five years later, their second child was born, a boy they named Santiago Leopoldo Sierra.

A product of capricious youth, the cynicism of the world challenged Salvatore and

Charlotte's love, and their marriage was swiftly plagued with abuses of every kind. Despite it all, Salvatore always made sure their venomous quarrels never poisoned his loving relationship with his children. Charlotte did not share her husband's honorable stance and was solely demonstrative toward their son, Santiago. After their love dwindled to childish regrets, pride solely sustained their marriage, and time matured their mutual hatred to cruel passion. The delicate façade of their marriage eventually deteriorated with the death of their son, Charlotte's single love, at the age of eight. Shortly thereafter, they finally divorced, and Charlotte left their hometown before the black ink properly and permanently dried their names over the paper.

In the following years, Charlotte would keep up the masquerade of dutiful mother entirely out of moral obligation and socialite vanity, visiting her daughter sparsely on birthdays and holidays. Miss Sierra always dreads these visits, these shallow rituals of propriety and civility. They are reliably spent in angst and with impassive verbal exchanges. Yet, it is no mystery to Miss Sierra as to why Charlotte reserves much hatred towards her. And at times of vulnerability and depression, Miss Sierra often wishes it were she who died in the tower that one odd winter rather than Santiago.

No matter how many years have come and gone, Miss Sierra's loathsomeness has never fully withered away to the ash. And even after so many years, Miss Sierra can still remember the rotting, wet stench of her little brother's corpse.

"Are you alright, Miss Sierra?" Bloodstone asks worriedly.

"Huh?" Miss Sierra's eyes flutter in confusion. She breaks free from the sting of bygone wounds with a soft sigh. "I—I've never taken the subway before. Just some ridiculous childhood phobia, really. Not sure if I'm ready to face it just yet, to be quite honest."

"Balderdash! Spontaneity and impulsion define adventure. We can never truly be ready for anything, Miss Sierra, and cowardice only hinders our growth." Bloodstone walks up to Miss Sierra. He pays no attention to her blanch complexion and hooks her with a muscular right arm to push her forward. "And we are made of sterner stuff, my dear. We are not ones to lull in the tranquility of our fears. No. We embrace fear itself, bark it into submission and become its master, for we are conquerors and warriors. Death itself shudders with anger at the mere mention of our names, for we mock it with fearless laughter." Bloodstone then lets off a bombastic laugh.

The Masked Philanthropist's laugh pierces the winds with the force of a sonic boom, and it proves to be quite contagious. Miss Sierra's phobias quickly recede to the void of childhood memory, purged from the present in gleeful giggles. It will be a moment to look back on with fondness. On this day, in the backdrop of a seedy neighborhood riddled with graffiti and a choir of barking dogs and purring alley cats, Bloodstone teaches Miss Sierra to be fearless.

CHAPTER 4

A TELLTALE BIRTHMARK

The subway entrance lies three blocks away from Alaska's Roshambo Café, and Dirty Southsville has seen better days. Yet the borough's decay somehow offers its impoverished residents a semblance of hope, and the distinguishable chirp of rambunctious children injects the otherwise barren wastelands with life and the promise of prosperity. Miss Sierra takes the opportunity and asks Bloodstone why he has not used his vast resources and wealth to restore the eroding community, what he responds with wigwags between noble practicality and neurosis.

For a time, Bloodstone considered

demolishing the borough to modernize it, but the effort had been bogged down with towers of paperwork, nagging demands for permits, and bitter contractor disputes. The Masked Philanthropist eventually grew disenchanted with the venture when his corporate phone and mailroom were plagued with endless city and bureaucratic citations of which he has little or moderate understanding. In the end, Bloodstone found it far more beneficial to purchase the borough's largest and most impoverished residential area, Mango Street, as a corporate property that would provide cheap housing for the less fortunate citizens of Cuckoo Meadows.

They swerve past a band of boys. They play around a water-sputtering fire hydrant and splash on the swelling puddles with a titter.

"Besides," Bloodstone exhales with a charitable pitch, "after taking an intimate look around these ancient streets and dwelling within its derelict walls, I couldn't bring myself to crumble a single building in the end. What wondrous tales would these decrepit, world-weary buildings tell us if only they could talk. They are monuments to the impoverished barrio I grew up in as a lad. Sentimentality won me over Miss Sierra, much to the chagrin of my board members."

"I can imagine. There can't be much profit in maintaining these, well, relics of a bygone memory." Miss Sierra adds purely. Though she openly doubts Bloodstone is the immortal he proclaims, nonetheless, she begins to understand why the public adores him. He acts like a modern-day folk hero.

"None whatsoever. Thousands are lost yearly. If only my board members would be immortal rather than I. Only then would they understand the bitter taste of eternity and learn that spirited memories are the true wealth of life, not gold or silver or cash equity." Bloodstone said bitterly.

"Well, I find it a most noble effort, Mister Bloodstone. A small sacrifice on your part, I'm sure, that helps hundreds, if not thousands of people, nonetheless. And no doubt the reason why the people worship you as some sort of a hero."

"A hero, me? Heavens no. I'm no hero, not at all." Bloodstone chuckles at the foolish notion. "Heroism is greatly overrated and often misconstrued as being synonymous with altruism, golden morality, and free of compromise. A noble dream, to be a hero. But I'm no dream Miss Sierra, just a man. Fallible, complex, and though ruggedly handsome underneath this silky mask, just as capable of humane ugliness as anyone else."

"You have a very low opinion of yourself, Mister Bloodstone." Miss Sierra said with a bemused smile. His humility is most charming to her.

They finally reach the underground subway entrance. Miss Sierra's knees buckle in protest, and she takes in a deep, shaky breath. Fortunately, Bloodstone is empathetic toward her phobia and holds her hand firmly. His hand is coarse and strong like stone yet paradoxically gentle. She smiles back at him, and both descend onto the metropolis's concrete belly. An unexplained alluring bond, free of romantic entanglements, suddenly ties Miss Sierra to the Masked Philanthropist—a platonic friendship forges between the two, a friendship sealed by their locking hands.

As they reach the ticket booth, Miss Sierra reaches for her coin purse with alarm. She prays the Masked Philanthropist does not take notice of her worry.

Her fingertips paw the interior woolen seams of her tiny coin purse, nothing. Miss Sierra's heart wants to jump out from her throat.

She can almost hear it, her mother's cruel laughter. She is without a dime or penny to pay for her boarding ticket. Miss Sierra's earlier hunger bled out her meager finances dry. Not even a cluster of lint is attached to her name now.

Bloodstone stands beside her and cocks an eyebrow. He studies her fruitless attempts to pluck a dime out from her bare purse with modest amusement. Aware of her dire financial straits and perplexed with admiration for her humble pride, the Masked Philanthropist pulls out his own gluttonous wallet and, without consideration for Miss Sierra's obvious embarrassment, pays for both their boarding tickets.

"No, wait. What are you doing?" Miss Sierra protests and chases Bloodstone through the spinning metal-barred door. She has never been comfortable in moments of obvious vulnerability and unjustly misinterprets Bloodstone's kind gesture. "Mister Bloodstone, I am more than capable of paying for my ticket, and I don't need you to rescue me again from a tight bind."

"Is that so, Miss Sierra? Because from where I stood, your pockets seemed barren and, dare I say, scarce of even lint." Bloodstone continues to march forward and flips a silver dollar into the guitar case of a blind man who plays an arrhythmic tune. "There's no need for you to feel shame after such a hapless conundrum. It happens to the best of us. Besides, my intention was not to heighten your feelings of desperation and inadequacy. I merely wanted to extend a friendly, helping hand to one in need."

"Inadequacy?!" She hisses angrily. "Now that remark there is boorishly bold, Mister Bloodstone, and tasteless, I might add. To think I figured you to be a gentleman."

Truth be told, Bloodstone's remarks, though on the dot and inoffensive, have struck a most sensitive, volatile nerve within Miss Sierra. It is a most unfortunate coincidence Bloodstone's sincere observations singe with the acidic voice of her beloved mother, whose oft-barbaric expectations have conditioned Miss Sierra's pride and ego to take offense to any sort of harmless observations.

"I'm not one to twist an arm for an apology, but I am confident one is due this instant."— she chides with a stomping foot.

Bloodstone stops at the heels of his boots, a few steps away from the corner of the subway platform. He tilts his masked head backward to examine Miss Sierra with a microscopic eye, keen to dwell through the labyrinthine corridors of her soul.

And he is most excited to discover the true woman hiding behind the cloak of insecurity.

Then, with a barking laugh, Bloodstone blankets her rage with mystified levity.

"You are quite the stubborn little firecracker, my dear." Bloodstone chortles. "Not many would dare take such an ill-advised stance or tone with me, why I could easily snap your neck but with two of my fingers alone. But to do so would not be incredibly wise of me, would it? I'd only be harming the one being courageous enough not to fear me. A sincere demonstration of respect, the purest I've met in years. You are quite right, Miss Sierra. An apology is due. Once again, please, accept my humblest apologies. It seems these past few decades have dulled my social etiquette. Now, are we good?"

"Y-Yes . . . we're good." Miss Sierra's eyes quiver with unease. *Did he just make a subtle threat at me?*—she wonders.

As Miss Sierra wrangles betwixt fear and flattery, a much fiercer voice grounds her thoughts back to the reality of the matter. Though Bloodstone, the Masked Philanthropist, is a well renowned public figure, he remains largely an enigmatic force. Nothing truly tactile is known about who or what he is nor from where he originates. To echo Robbie's—the fiery redhead newscaster—morning appraisal, though the world recognizes Bloodstone the C.E.O., Bloodstone the Philanthropist, and Bloodstone the Storyteller, no one has ever perceived the true Bloodstone—the man underneath the mask.

The subterranean train's metallic shriek echoes softly behind the tunnel's curtain of shadows. A gust of mechanized breath blows past them to pronounce the subway train's timely arrival. The shrieking gears go mute over the thumping footsteps, and droplets of electric sparks halt the worm-like train. The doors slide open and, without warning, forms zigzag in a stampeding blur. The exiting and entering commuters flounder elbow to buttocks before the doors shut them out. The afternoon commune is light; they are still hours away from the evening rush. Bloodstone and Miss Sierra enter the subway car. The doors slide shut behind them, and, in a forceful push, they are set on their way.

Miss Sierra's wristwatch reads one-fifteen in the afternoon, and Sugar Hill Pier is a short five stops away. They will make their destination right on the last ticking second.

Miss Sierra, much to her surprise, is quite relaxed throughout the entire ride. But as a precaution not to relapse on her phobias, she entertains herself and examines the squalor who boggle about the car, all of whom lead slothful, parasitic lives.

They are the undesirable dregs of Cuckoo Meadows. Undoubtedly, they ride the subway with no intended destination except to kill time.

The more ambitious and morally inclined citizenry are hard at work with their day jobs, working to outlive the great social degeneration plaguing the world. All while the oligarchy looks down upon the rest with smug disdain, believing themselves the heirs—the new gods—of an undeserving and deformed world. Such is the cynical views of her homely father, who has fought hard to purge all sort of smutty ambitions of adventure and self-gratification from his politely rebellious daughter. In time, he eventually recognized his efforts were no more than naïve attempts to control his daughter—a daughter who slowly sheds away from the chrysalis of childhood and is more than ready to careen through the more turbulent affairs of an unjust world. He did not approve of Miss Sierra's decision to leave for Cuckoo Meadows, what he considers a modern-day Sodom and Gomora. Regardless, he silently applauds her otherwise meek valor for taking control of her own destiny. His tears spoke of sadness but gleamed with pride. A fact of which Miss Sierra is still not privy.

"Who exactly is this contact of yours?" Miss Sierra asks. She unfastens her scarf, allowing her neck to finally breathe. The subway car is much warmer, and the incubating space has made her perspire lightly. The few dozen bodies surrounding them give further rise to the boiling heat.

"One of my Pulque Bunnies. Old boy goes by the name of Macario. He's a queer-looking fellow, and with an odd appetite for the discarded leftovers of others. You might've had a run-in with him a time or two digging through your trash cans and paid him no attention. He's quite harmless, I assure you, and his uncanny taste buds will prove beneficial to our mission." Bloodstone said with weighted truthfulness, unaware he has raised more questions.

"Mister Bloodstone, you do know I'm still

somewhat of a stranger to Cuckoo Meadows. You might as well speak in riddles because I'm having a difficult time understanding just about everything you've said." Miss Sierra is unsure if Bloodstone speaks in metaphors or in some sort of urban slang. None of it makes sense to her. She quietly demands clarity with a lifted eyebrow and puckered lips.

"Quite the greenhorn, I see. Very well then, Miss Sierra, your guide to this fair gem that is Cuckoo Meadows, I shall be. These Pulque Bunnies are my eyes and ears to things which I may be blind and deaf. To you and others less imaginative, they are a trio of good-natured and naïve vagrants. But the telltale antlers sprouting at the top of their skulls always gives them away—them being Macario, Block, and Anton. When I resurfaced and settled back to Cuckoo Meadows, some thirty-odd years ago—I believe—all three rediscovered me and resumed their pledge of eternal fealty; 'tis a life debt, you see, joyously owed after I rescued them from the sinister machinations of inter-dimensional, bodiless, living brains centuries ago." Bloodstone locks eyes with Miss Sierra. His tale is beyond sound reason; thus, it merits scowling conviction. "Makes me feel young again to remember such a bizarre adventure, the first of many. Now, if I can only remember the exact when? Hmm, I believe it happened way back in '65. No, no, that doesn't sound right—ah, yes! Yes, '62 it was back in '62, way back in 1962 if memory proves reliable."

"Sounds like a romantic tale of swashbuckling hijinks. I look forward to hearing it in its entirety in the future, Mister Bloodstone." Miss Sierra finds no point in questioning the validity of Bloodstone's story. She has quickly learned this much for the moment. The eerie steadiness in Bloodstone's voice isn't what dissuades her from challenging his apparent delicate sanity. No. It is the glinting spark in his eyes that, oddly, makes Miss Sierra question her sanity instead. But 1962, over two hundred years ago, that is preposterous—impossible!

Isn't it?

"Here's a curious thought." She continues. "If they are your eyes and ears in the shadows— this trio of, um, Pulque Bunnies—then how come they haven't come forward with the thieves' identity? Then again, I imagine even bunnies of queer nature must blink for moisture occasionally."

"Ah yes, well, you see the thing is,"

Bloodstone rubs the nape of his neck. He gives the appearance of a child who grows ashamed after wetting his pants. "They normally guard my residence and vault in my absence, obviously. But on that day, I decided, um, to give them the day off."

"You gave them the day off . . .?" Miss Sierra repeats with a wry chuckle. It is an amusing lapse in judgment to leave his coveted vault without a guard. Moreover, the circumstances of the theft itself are so normal, especially considering Bloodstone's abnormal pith. Bloodstone joins Miss Sierra in the giggles, at which point a notion tickles Miss Sierra's suspicions. "Mister Bloodstone, wouldn't anyone else within your staff have known about your Pulque Bunnies?"

"Not really. Only my closest aides would know such a delicate fact." Bloodstone responds with puzzlement.

"I think it is obvious then—there is a traitor within your inner circle."—she concludes sternly.

"Hmm . . . that is most troubling. Yes, troubling indeed. Only four individuals enjoy the boon of my trust. All of whom have been under my employment for five or more years.

More tragically, they've each bonded with me over death-defying adventures." Bloodstone broods to himself. The idea of a serpentine individual slithering its poisonous hide amidst his organization is a perverse and intolerable insult to Bloodstone. He squeezes the metal handrail and snaps it off like a dried-up twig. A demonic breath seethes between his gnashing teeth when he finally speaks again. "Pray for the misguided soul who has dared to pierce my noble heart, Miss Sierra. Best they have already fled Cuckoo Meadows for their sake, or they shall learn that to play games of deception with me is to play games of death."

Loyalty is a sacred commandment to Bloodstone. Trust is measured not in trivial abstractions like time or love. But akin to sacrificing one's purity of the flesh to another soul. To betray such a sacrifice is a blasphemous encroachment on the vulnerabilities entrusted to the betrayer. The Masked Philanthropist's peak physical perfection lives up to the stone half of his name. But even stone itself can be shattered to oblivion. Bloodstone's heart has been wounded, and he is unashamed to let his glum emotions pour out from his eyes in streams of tears. He would later tell Miss Sierra that his pain necessitated the rain of tears, for he has no desire to dwell in what will become plaintive scars. In time, the still unknown offender will reap brutal retribution at Bloodstone's sinuous, hammer-like fists. Vengeance repaid in blood; the Immortal Luchador sees it fit to live up to the other half of his name.

"It'll be alright, Mister Bloodstone. You can rest easy tonight. I will never betray you. I'd much rather die first before considering such a suicidal thing." Miss Sierra reaches out to Bloodstone's hand without hesitation.

This time around, it is she who comes to his rescue. Her pure and true touch fills the imposing Masked Philanthropist with a warmness he has long forgotten. He smiles.

The subway train reaches its first stop. The time now reads one-twenty, and Miss Sierra starts to doubt they will make their destination to Sugar Hill Pier on time. The next wave of crowds starts to board the car. This time around, it is of a greater noise and unpleasantness. Businessmen plugged to their mobile phones, hobos bathed in their urine, and truant teenagers snickering and whiffing a stick of Evergreen Blaze, trot, and wallop about without a care, much less consideration for the other passengers.

The snickering teens bump against Miss Sierra's back—she thinks one might have groped her bum—and the subway car tugs forward again. The sudden movement surprises Miss Sierra, and she losses her footing. She topples forward, and her medium-length hair is brushed to the side. To her relief, Bloodstone grabs her by the arm. She is spared the horror of having her face brush up against the countless pieces of gum, among other stains, that infests the subway car's grungy floor. Miss Sierra's neck is exposed during the short tussle, and, with wide-eyed concern, the Masked Philanthropist makes a shocking discovery just below the right side of her neckline.

There is an area of melted flesh with a mark emblazoned on her skin that resembles an eight-pointed star, much like a raging sun bleeding through the sky. The melted, scarred flesh tells a forgotten tale involving a hot, steaming branding iron. Whether it is a memento from a cruel childhood prank taken too far or the marking of a tortured soul is uncertain, but Bloodstone is committed to finding out.

"My dear, what is this marking so vulgarly

etched just below your neck?" Bloodstone asks with raging concern.

"What . . .? What do you mean?" Miss Sierra's cheeks flush pink with humiliation when she notices what Bloodstone refers to. Shakily, she brushes her hair back in place and conceals the vulgar scar. She has never felt such nude vulnerability. "Oh . . . it—it's just a scar. Not quite the pretty little flower, is it? I would appreciate it if you'd not stare at it, Mister Bloodstone. It's not something I openly talk about with just anyone. Being it's a scar, it's a permanent reminder of my poor judgment, among other unpleasantries. I'd much like to remain oblivious to its existence."

"Who gave you that mark? Give me a name, at the very least. And I will see to it that the monster responsible is bled dry for having harmed you so perversely." Bloodstone's fists clench stiff with bloodlust, and behind the ivory mask, several veins crack above his right brow. He tolerates a great many things, but betrayal and, most of all, the abuse and disrespect towards a lady, are sins he deems unforgivable.

"I consider you a respectable man, Mister Bloodstone." Miss Sierra shies away from his stern glower. "And I'm appreciative of your chivalry, but as I had mentioned before—I'm in no need of any kind of saving. I trust you can respect this."

She is unaccustomed to such nobility. Not that her father isn't a noble man himself, but Bloodstone simply appears more ancient, even Arthurian. Miss Sierra has always considered herself a lone star among a cluster of stars. Similar in appearance to the rest, but with a different kind of fire burning deep at the core. It makes her unique, a lone oddity best shunned and ignored. Yet, here stands this nebulous stranger, an oddity much like herself, demonstrating her a rare kind of friendship.

Miss Sierra's lips quiver with shame when she continues. "Besides, you—you're already looking at the monster responsible. I'd hoped you would've discovered this little ugliness of mine sometime down the future, instead of the present."

"What was it you said to me earlier?—Ah yes. You have an incredibly low opinion of yourself, Miss Sierra. We are all ugly in some way, though there are those of us who let that ugliness define us. Do not be fooled by my godly features. Behind this epitome of masculinity, you see, lies an ugliness which, unlike aged wine, has become more grotesque. And should you ever take a small glimpse, count yourself fortunate if you should only suffer the comforts of nightmares afterward." Bloodstone gently tilts Miss Sierra's head back up. They lock gazes. "We are all imperfect creatures capable of great beauty. Therein lies the beauty of our imperfection. Now, tell me, whatever compelled you to desecrate yourself in such a profane matter?"

"I—I don't know." Miss Sierra replies and nervously brushes her hair.

"Come now. You swore to always be honest with me." Bloodstone protests firmly.

Miss Sierra has buried such a traumatic memory for good reason. The tiniest details allude her like the finer grains of a photograph erased by the rasp of time. She closes her eyes, sees herself, a little girl, age five. White snow softly blankets her hometown, and her parents are truly in love, for the last time. Through the haze of winter, she recalls her mother's angry shriek like shattering ice. Integrity soils her father's honor, and the branding iron's sizzling taunts her. The scar beckons the pains of yesterday, and she remembers how the burn paled to the venomous sting whenever her mother refers to her as the usurper. The melted star is a constant reminder of when the title of daughter was denied to her, and the warmth of a mother's love was snuffed with the winds of winter.

There is no avoiding the past now. No matter how painful, it is all transcribed in blood and betrayal over the parchment which chronicles her life. But as far as Miss Sierra is concerned, the details of the past can often be read for reflection and never ingrained beyond the immaterial.

Miss Sierra opens her eyes and shares the scar's tale with the Masked Philanthropist with purity.

"I am an adopted child, Mister Bloodstone. I—I was only five when my father told my mother a—about her stillborn child. I was five when I learned I had usurped their trueborn child's life, legacy, and love. I was never meant to overhear any of it, though." Miss Sierra recites stolidly. The past can often be like a hundred-handed specter that constantly claws at her back. But Miss Sierra never answered its tiresome mewling. She always refused it. *Why am I telling him this?*—she asks herself. Perhaps the Masked Philanthropist's pride and chivalry inspires her to confess her sins freely.

"It all happened because of a stupid birthmark. You see, my mother comes from a prideful bloodline, the Foix Bloodline. And every member of the Foix clan is born w— with an eight-pointed star-shaped birthmark, usually in the region of the right shoulder, near the base of the neck. My, um, my mother bears the mark, as did her father and his father and so on. My mother used to tell me to bear the mark of the Foix was a great honor, back when she saw me as a daughter. Back when she thought me to be her flesh and blood.

She noticed my birthmark was absent. Naturally, she got concerned. I can still hear the horrific, mad shrill she let off when my father told her the truth about their stillborn child. A child who still lies buried somewhere out there in the mountains, deep in the dirt and snow. I ran out to our barn, where the oxen slept, tears trickling down my rosy cheeks. I was as heartbroken as my mother was from the revelation when I noticed the warm hum of the branding iron. And so, I decided to give myself the birthmark my mother longed for because I wanted her to see me as her real daughter again because I desperately wanted her to love me again."

"Blood alone does not define family, Miss

Sierra. It goes much deeper. And the love that comes with it, well, it is like a sweet and poisonous liquor—intoxicating to the point where soundness goes numb and good judgment unseen." Bloodstone's long, storied past leeches his voice, and it trails away. Unlike Miss Sierra, he is not quite ready to share it. He sighs heavily and continues. "Our story together has merely begun, and we still many wondrous and bizarre adventures ahead of us, yet you've already vowed your trust and loyalty to me. So, it is only fair I do the same. Miss Sierra, I solemnly swear to uphold our friendship with the same righteous fealty and bittersweet annoyances of family."

"You truly are a noble and strange man, Mister Bloodstone." Miss Sierra said with a warm smile. "I am officially touched. Am I to be your little sister then?"

"More like a little-big sister." Bloodstone laughs back. "For you'll soon learn I have a child-like penchant for mischief and a terrible habit to mock Death itself."

The subway train reaches its second stop. Trotting footsteps go in and out. The doors slide shut, and the rail wheels shriek onward. There are still three more stops before they reach Sugar Hill Pier.

CHAPTER 5

QUEER RENDEZVOUS WITH BUNNIES

Sugar Hill Pier makes up Cuckoo Meadows' entire westside bay, and it is the most economically rich of the four boroughs that make up the metropolis. The cool, sandy beaches are always sparkling with life, and the borough is renowned for its fine diners. The most popular being Wamblee Whale's Shrimp Boat, Bluebonnet's Butchered Cow, and Huan Wu's Gun Pow Chicken. For fluff, sugary pastries, caramelized candies, milk chocolatey sweets, and lush rainbow palettes of ice cream, there is the world-renown purveyor of sweets, Bubble Gum Gumbo's Ice Cream Parlor. The borough also offers family-friendly fare with Umiko

Rompopo's Aquarium and the bodacious theme park attraction, Gigi's Supercalifragilistic Imaginarium, is rarely scarce of roaring, jubilant laughter. The crystalline beauty of Sugar Hill Pier is uncanny, save for Macario—the oddball vagrant who happens to be one of Bloodstone's queer Pulque Bunnies.

Hands deep in a trash can, Macario busies himself scurrying for food through the discarded filth while he impatiently waits for Bloodstone and his newly appointed assistant. "Hungry, so very, very hungry. People like to waste good grubs. So sad to waste 'em good grubs on maggots. Something will pop. I know it 'cause people always like to waste good grubs."—the humble vagrant mumbles to no one.

His fingers caress something moist and squishy, and Macario greedily hoists it out from the waste. His eyes glitter with glee and surprise, the peppy Pulque Bunny has scored a half-eaten hotdog smudged with a thin glace of yucky tang. Macario hops around giddily and then takes a whiff of the mucky hotdog with his short-pointy nose. Passersby pay him no respectable attention; they are too afraid to provoke his foxy, cartoon wackiness and the pair of double-pronged horns that sprout from under his hoodie do not quite inspire friendliness either. But none of it bothers Macario. All he needs in life to be happy is his freedom, his friends Block, Anton, and Bloodstone, his shopping cart full of plugged glass bottles (bottles whose arcane nature is unknown to everyone except a Pulque Bunny), his grungy meals and bottles of booze.

Macario shoves the hotdog whole in his mouth. His cheeks fluff while he munches on the soiled hotdog, and he then washes down the chewed chunks with a full bottle of golden-brown whiskey. The liquor's spell holds no sway over Macario's senses. Inebriation is an alien affliction to Macario and his brethren, much like they themselves are aliens of sorts to Cuckoo Meadows and the modern world.

Macario dusts the crumbs off his faded, stained blue jeans jacket and scrunches up the left sleeve up. He examines the collection of wristwatches that tick in synchrony to the millisecond. His tiny, round eyes almost bulge out of their sockets when he sees each watch tick closer to 1:25 p.m. "Late, oh dear, he's late. Boss is never late. Bad, something bad—terrible—must've happened."

Macario is unaware Bloodstone's tardiness is a tad minutes long. Shotgun Joe's earlier antics have held up the Masked Philanthropist longer than he initially thought. A stickler for punctuality, Macario anxiously wiggles his short-pointy nose to catch a whiff of Bloodstone's odor in the drifting ambient air. Once he does, he then pierces the empty air with a finger. Macario summons his inborn magicks and tears a hole open in the air that strobes with blue magicks. He leans backward, jumps into the blueish dimensional tear, and swiftly disappears along with it.

The few spectators who witness the event brush off the oddness as a trick of the eye, a heat-induced mirage. Self-indulgent falsehood, 'tis the truth. There is no heat haze to gaslight the eye and mind, only the chilled kiss of a forthcoming winter.

<hr>

"I don't think we're going to make it to Sugar Hill Pier on time, Mister Bloodstone." Miss Sierra said to an unconcerned Bloodstone. "We are still two stops away, and it's already five till one-thirty. You don't suppose your contact will wait for us?"

"No, not likely. Old Mackie has never been the most patient of creatures. As a matter of fact, he will most likely overthink this minor tardiness and believe me to be in some sort of danger." Bloodstone examines their surroundings expectantly, prepping for what is to come next. The overhead lights suddenly flicker. Miss Sierra assumes it to be a minor electrical hiccup. Bloodstone knows better, and she has yet to learn to expect the unexpected. "Ah Mackie, you predictable, peevish little bunny. Miss Sierra, be so kind and grab on to me. Oh, and fear not what you are about to witness. It is merely old Mackie making his grand entrance."

"Okay . . . I'm not sure I understand what's—" the sudden shudder of a stirring quake cuts Miss Sierra short.

The lights flicker madly, like a nervous shudder of the eye. Miss Sierra grabs hold of Bloodstone's right arm and wraps both her arms around it. The lights' flicker grows more violent, and light and shadow skip at a quicker pace. The other passengers remain completely oblivious to the electrical seizure blanketing them. Miss Sierra's foolishness soon disappears along with the other passengers. Now it is only she and Bloodstone who remain riding inside a vacant car. She thinks her own eyes deceive her. At the far end of the car, a strange and ghostly anomaly slowly shears away the invisible and untouchable air. The gaping hole strobes with blue light that gently warps the fabric of reality. The phenomenon leaves Miss Sierra agape with shock, whilst Bloodstone remains utterly unimpressed. The hole's blue strobe continues to ripple the ambient air and sets off swelling rings as if over a calm spring. Bloodstone and Miss Sierra go unaffected from the magickal ripple, even after all color is siphoned dry. Everything reverts to pure blacks and whites and greys. What remains sane are a mere two insignificant stains of color potted within a grey waste and in the company of a third, oddball blue stain.

The Pulque Bunny Macario has arrived.

"Hiya boss, you were a tad late. I got worried. Thought you were in great peril, maybe wrestling with the Death Gods at the undergloom." Macario said in a hangdog manner and blushed pink when he realizes Bloodstone is in no immediate danger. "I—I'm sorry, boss. It looks like I jumped the gun . . . again."

"Think nothing of it, Mackie old boy. I'm always touched by your jittery concern. But as you can see, your concern is wasted on jitters alone." Bloodstone replies. He moves to the side to reveal Miss Sierra, who has hidden behind him seconds before Macario's fashionable entrance. "Macario, I'd like you to meet the ever impressionable, sharp-tongued, and young beauty, Miss Sierra. She has recently been hired to be my new personal assistant, but from here on out, she is to be more. She is to be our friend."

"Pleasure to make your acquaintance, miss." Macario extends a thin, pale hand to Miss Sierra.

"Likewise," she replies, transfixed with his rabbity features, moreover, by the pair of two-pronged horns sprouting from the top of his head. Miss Sierra is curious about their organic or artificial grain. She cannot tell if they are real or not since the horns' roots remain concealed underneath the hoodie Macario hides most of his face.

"Boss, Block told me about the theft of your precious Black Fungi Beetle box. His heart aches heavy with terrible, terrible guilt for not having been there to prevent it." Macario wiggles his bony fingers in the air melodramatically. "He no longer considers himself worthy of your friendship or to serve you. Boss, you must talk to him, you must, he—he has left Cuckoo Meadows with that overgrown chicken from Mitla Street in a trail of tears. He didn't mean to dishonor you. None of us meant to. You have got to talk to him, boss. Get him to come back home, back to his family."

"He has done what?! Why would he leave with that old gargoyle?" Bloodstone said in an outburst of concern. The Masked Philanthropist takes a brief five seconds to meditate on the situation. Having lost one of his Pulque Bunnies—nay, they are something more. Having potentially lost one of his closest, oldest friends over a misunderstanding does not rest well with Bloodstone. They are, as Macario stated, family. "Mackie, I need both you and Anton to find and bring Block back home. That old bird won't be easily dissuaded into releasing him, so do what you must. Tell him—tell Block—he is not at fault. I gave him the day off, unaware there was a traitor in our midst. Can you do that for me, Mackie?"

"Yes, yes, of course, boss. Gotta get Block back home. World's too cruel and dangerous for bunnies like us. Especially here, where monsters often wear the face of friends."

Macario hops happily. "Old bird means well, boss, but we belong here with you."

"Indeed, you do, old boy. Now before you go hopping about, looking for dear wounded Block, I require the assistance of your keen taste buds. You think you can help me with this first, Mackie?" Bloodstone pulls out a rolled-up piece of paper from his leather jacket. He unrolls it and reveals a partially bitten, honey-glazed cube of chicken meat. "I personally inspected every corner of my vault. The thieves left behind no distinguishable fingerprints, hairs, nor droplets of sweat, save this chickeny morsel. I'd hoped to uncover its place of birth on my own. I was wrong to think so. Now, Mackie, old boy, tell me, who is the purveyor of this chicken cube."

Macario eagerly snatches the chicken cube off the Masked Philanthropist's hand and examines it with extreme scrutiny. The Pulque Bunny sniffs it with his short-pointy nose, licks it with the tip of his tongue, and smacks and moistens his lips with hungry anticipation. After the abnormal ritual, Macario flings the chicken cube into his mouth and quickly works to chew on it, suckling on its collage of succulent flavors.

Throughout the entire situation, Miss Sierra studies their ghostly enclosure. They are somewhere beyond the natural plane, that much she has figured out on her own. Which somewhere is beyond her realm of understanding. *What is this? Some sort of touchable dream?*—she toys with the absurd plausibility. *Nonsense, I'm fully awake—I think. Cuckoo Meadows is densely populated and industrialized. Yes, that's it. I must've inhaled too much of the pollutants that float in the city's air.*—she knows it foolish to think such an outlandish theory aloud. Deny, as she may the many implausible things which occur before her eyes, Miss Sierra realizes she lies isolated in an impotent mindset. She remains stock-still, without a sound voice to comprehend what her eyes refuse to let her unsee. But she does wonder—*what or who exactly is this old gargoyle?*

Macario continues to suckle on the chewed-up chicken cube. It is quite tasty. With eyes shut, Macario's talented taste buds do their work. The Pulque Bunny can read every single atom, both native and foreign, that composite and have touched the tiny morsel. From spices down to the very saliva drenched over it, Macario tastes it all with delicacy.

"Good, good, incredibly good. What's this I taste now?—oh yeah, a buttered-up sterling silver pan. Oh no. awfully bad—week-old butter and oil. Health Department won't like this one bit. Old Mackie don't mind, though. He likes week-old butter." Macario reports the first string of flavors with child-like giddiness. "Oh, there it is, boss' oily touch. Taste like coconut . . . Hm?—Bleh! Old chum who munched on this here Kung Pao Chicken got a bad case of the gingivitis. Now onto the chicken. Usual mix of oils, veggies, and . . . oh my, a special peanut was used here. Oh my, expensive too. Only one restaurant uses this special nut in their dishes. Boss, them jacking chickens be the thieves who stole your treasure."

"I should've known it was those cackling cocks. Only they possess the talents to break into my vault without a naked trace." Bloodstone said. He looks to Miss Sierra, who cocks him an inquisitive brow. "We have found our thieves, my dear. They are a gang of career thieves known as the Gong Bao Chicken Gang. And undoubtedly, someone far sinister hired them to perform the deed. We must track them down to their roost and get them to release the identity of the coup's true architect."

"That's good news, Mister Bloodstone, um, just—I mean . . ." Miss Sierra's words stutter out. She is still unable to comprehend the *grey zone* they themselves solely inhabit. "Okay. I don't exactly know where we are at right now. I suppose my question is—how do we get out of here?"

"Out of here?" Bloodstone repeats, somewhat confused. "Ah yes, *here*! Quite easily, Miss Sierra. Macario, if you would please release us from this time-lapse. We have an urgent appointment with the Gong Bao Chicken Gang."

Bloodstone cracks his knuckles in eager anticipation of the retribution to come. The Pulque Bunny nods obediently, and with a quick wiggle of his short-pointy nose, noise rings their ears, color is restored, and, to Miss Sierra's relief, they are once again among the living crowds.

"You've done well, as usual, Mackie. Now, go grab Anton and bring back home our Block." Bloodstone commands to the Pulque Bunny.

"Thank you, boss. Oh, thank you. He'll be

so relieved to know you ain't cross with him." Macario whimpers with joy. He then swings to Miss Sierra with an awkward grin. "And it was a pleasure to make your acquaintance, new friend."

"It was a most . . . interesting experience meeting you, Mister Pulque Bunny." Miss Sierra said with an awkwardness to match Macario's grin.

"Mackie will do, new friend."

"Mackie, it is then . . . new friend." Miss Sierra smiles warmly back to the queer Pulque Bunny.

There are many questions she wants to be answered, but, alas, it will all have to wait for another time. The subway car's doors slide open.

"Come, Miss Sierra, we have reached our destination," Bloodstone barks and rushes through the crowds.

How did we reach Sugar Hill Pier in the space of a few minutes?—another question screams at her without an answer to echo back. Miss Sierra rushes steadfast after Bloodstone. She takes a few paces onto the platform but turns quickly to wave goodbye to Macario one last time. To her surprise, Macario isn't there anymore. Instead, she only sees an adorable little brown jackrabbit with a pair of two-pronged horns sprouting a tad above its forehead. The jackrabbit looks back to her with its almond black eyes in equal fascination. Then, the little jackrabbit stands on its hind legs and waves a paw to her shortly before the doors slide shut between them.

Miss Sierra blinks in disbelief and laughs aloud. She swivels away and chases after Bloodstone. She brushes off the oddness as a trick of the eyes, a heat-induced mirage. But there is no heat haze to gaslight the eye and mind, only the chilled kiss of a forthcoming winter.

CHAPTER 6

THE GONG BAO CHICKEN (GANG) CREW

"Seven hours? How did we lose seven hours?" Miss Sierra gives a flummoxed scream. "This—how? We were only in that—that—whatever that void was, for a mere few minutes. Two minutes, to be exact."

Miss Sierra comes close to regurgitating her forenoon meal. When they finally reach the surface, twinkling stars and the blue moon greet her agape surprise. Her wristwatch clocks at one-thirty, yet it is already nighttime. The Masked Philanthropist is, like every madness before, unfazed with this mysterious theft of time by some otherworldly force. No doubt, experiences that tread on the strange and bizarre are nothing particularly exceptional to him, but to Miss Sierra, it is all a newborn sensation. She is unaccustomed to paranormal phenomenon that defy the very laws of nature and even the limitations of the human imagination.

Time has been compressed. A few hours have passed in a span of mere minutes. She has been robbed of seven hours, and a strutting portly man makes this fact concrete.

"Sir, could you please give me the time? My watch, it seems to be off by a few hours." She pleads to the man.

"Quarter till nine, sweetheart"—the portly man reports.

Somehow the unassuming creature, Macario the Pulque Bunny, has devoured the missing seven hours, and Miss Sierra demands an explanation for this vile intrusion upon her very soul.

"I demand an explanation Mister Bloodstone." Miss Sierra scorns. "What happened to the seven missing hours of my life?"—she adds, wrangling with her unweaving grasp on reality. She fails to notice that Bloodstone's mind is adrift over other more selfish concerns.

Bloodstone's hard, brooding glower gleams with deep thoughts of retribution and dark resolve. More than before, he is determined to reclaim his stolen treasure at any cost, even if it necessitates bludgeoning the skull of every Gong Bao Chicken Gang member down to a bloodied pool of brain matter. Suppose the Gong Bao Chicken Gang had stolen any other artifact from his vault, any of which would have turned up a reasonable profit in the black market. In that case, the Masked Philanthropist might have overlooked the theft for a harmless prank pioneered by a pack of hungry youngbloods trying to earn their bones as legitimate and fearless thieves. But the impetuous fools have made a fatal mistake pilfering Bloodstone's prized black box. It was a gift from the Pulque Bunny Anton, carved out from the husk of a Black Fungi Beetle—a rare creature native to Dimension X, itself laced with a storied history—and shelters the one possession Bloodstone holds uniquely golden above all others.

Bloodstone is over two hundred years old, and within those two minuscule centuries, he has accumulated a great many hollow mementos from bygone and oft-forgotten lives. That is the gauge of these "riches" greedily tucked away inside his skyrise vault, shallow memories of a non-existent individual. So why is this little black box any different?

"It was that Pulque Bunny fellow, wasn't it? He did something. I can't explain what he did, but I know this—this insanity is his doing." Miss Sierra continues, oblivious to Bloodstone's bleeding heart.

"Hm?" Bloodstone turns. Miss Sierra's voice reminds him that he is not alone in this adventure. "Can you run that over me again, Miss Sierra?"

Miss Sierra bites down her lips and then stomps her foot down. Her eyes bleed hot with piqued rage. She puffs her cheeks like a scorned lover and lets out an understandable, crazed shriek.

"Forgive me, Miss Sierra. I—I'm still unaccustomed to another's company. For far too long, the only company I've had are my thoughts." Bloodstone sighs with a weighty breath. "Hundreds of chirping voices may swirl around me on the daily, but you are the first voice I've truly heard in over fifty years. Not even my Pulque Bunnies share that privilege."

"If you hear my voice as you claim, then

please, Mister Bloodstone, explain this—this anomaly to me. How did we jump from early afternoon to early night in a short breath?" Miss Sierra asks more calmly. "Up to this point, I've taken everything you've said to me in good faith. I'll admit, I don't really believe you to be the immortal you claim to be, and I don't buy into the hype surrounding your lavish and renowned tall tales. But right now, I find myself somewhat afraid—afraid for my own sanity. Don't bother asking for the why. I'll simply tell you this instant—before this madness fully consumes my mind. I'm afraid—afraid that I'm finding myself questioning my existence because of what—whatever that Macario fellow did was not normal. I find the whole thing perversely unsettling. Was it . . . normal? And are we all nothing more than dreams then?"

"Dreams are only as real as we want them to be, Miss Sierra. Question, not your existence. Rather, question how you can make the most of it. Welcome, Miss Sierra, to the moonshine that is our existence. Where dreams themselves laugh, cry and love as we do." Bloodstone continues with conscious sensibility. He has no desire to plunge her mind into the void of insanity. "Now hush those screams in your mind child, it is normal to obsess over one's tangibility after venturing through Macario's *Grey Warren*. It's nothing more than a pocket dimension or bubble of sorts, where time collapses to a paused singularity. Unlike Anton, Mackie, unfortunately hasn't fully mastered the simultaneous transportation of multiple bodies. Hence, our missing hours. He has gotten much better, though. Before, he would've thrust us weeks ahead. Look at the bright side, though, Miss Sierra. We are technically seven hours younger than the rest of the world. Ha-ha-ha!"

"Pocket dimensions? Compressed time? This—this is too much. I need to sit down." Miss Sierra sits at the sidewalk's curb. Her thoughts spin her into a daze, and she gazes up to the spindly trees. The winter winds have unburdened their stress, and they dance naked of the autumn oranges, yellows, and reds. She envies the trees, whose shoulders stress over little, mundane things like leaves. "I—I'm sorry, Mister Bloodstone, but I'm afraid I can't go forward with you on this journey. I much prefer to deal with the madness of loons like Shotgun Joe. At least I can pretend to understand his type of madness. This other madness, though—it's just too plain weird for my taste."

"No," Bloodstone replies with a stonelike authority.

"No . . .? I'm sorry, you misunderstood what I've just said. It wasn't a request. I'm resigning right here on the spot—I quit. I don't want the job anymore. Sorry, I wasted your time. Period." Miss Sierra rebuffs indignantly.

"You don't realize it now, Miss Sierra, but you've reaffirmed my reasons for having chosen you as my personal assistant in the first place. Reasons I shan't explain. You see, I have great faith that you'll figure it out on your own by the day's end." Bloodstone leans and sits to join her at the curb. He assures to hold her in his gaze with sincere humility. "And this has become more than just a working relationship, remember? We are together to the end in this newborn friendship. Our time together as of now may only be brief, but I like to believe you of a sharp mind, courageous, adventurous, and one never to abandon a friend in need. Tell me then, my dear, am I wrong to have made such assumptions of you?"

Friendship, the very word, is a cipher to her. As a child, the other children shunned her for reasons that still allude her to this day. They probably sensed something vulgar festering within her. A something the adults were blind to see. Perhaps it was the inherited innocence of children that made them more sensitive to the bohemian rhythm of her soul. Whatever this impurity was that incited their fears and hatred towards her, eventually faded along with her springs, and her past has now become a forgotten winter. She has accepted the possibility of never experiencing the kindness of foreign hearts, much less the joyful pains of friendship.

And quite understandably, it comes of no surprise Bloodstone's pleas reach out to the heart whose saddened cries spiral barren through an empty seashell.

Bloodstone and Miss Sierra, their shared aloneness, unknowingly bonds them further and stronger.

"No. You're not wrong, Mister Bloodstone." She answers softly.

"Rarely I am so, Miss Sierra," Bloodstone replies cockily.

They share a short laugh. Bloodstone rises to his feet, and, in a gentlemanly display, he offers a hand to Miss Sierra. She accepts the kind gesture and gets back up on her feet. Levity resumes, and both continue to stride down the pier along the road that divides the lavish condominiums from the sandy beaches beside them.

<hr>

To common folk, Cooks Corpus Drive is a renowned Cuckoo Meadows landmark since the city's inception back in 1907. An emporium housing a myriad of colorful food vendors who provide the great majority of the city's restaurants with fresh vegetables, fruits, nuts, spices, oils, and the meats of every beast imaginable. The historic alley also brings chefs from the world over together in an exchange of culinary secrets wherein their creative cuisines are blended to create an entirely new, savory dish.

Early mornings, just before the sun washes the blues of the night away, are the most hectic hours at Cooks Corpus Drive. Should you ever visit the alley between the early hours of 3:00 a.m. and 5:00 a.m., you are likely to hear crass hooting from the city's collective of prestigious and often bitter rivaling restaurateurs who fight tooth and claw over the freshest of ingredients. Propriety and civility have no place in the savage world of the chef, especially if you wish to enslave the appetites of the public with the aroma of your seductive and delicious meals.

More so if you wish for your restaurant to thrive in Cuckoo Meadows' competitive market. In the end, the taste will always win you the loyalty of the public, and victory always starts with the freshest of ingredients.

Though the alley is fairly known for its congregation of embattled chefs, the alley is foremost known as home to one of Sugar Hill Pier's premier restaurants, Huan Wu's Gun Pow Chicken. Of course, details of the sort regarding Cooks Corpus Drive can always be read about in travel vouchers made readily available to the more civilized folk at any of Cuckoo Meadows' travel agencies or hotels and resorts. After all, Cooks Corpus Drive has many facets, most of which aren't as benign. No, to the more street-savvy citizenry of Cuckoo Meadows, the alley is seen for what it truly is—a cesspool infested with a far more ravenous breed of a scavenger than the common warrior-chef or persecuted sewer rat. To the outcasts and unwanted scum of society, the alley is more commonly known as Crooks Corporate Drive. A far less noncancerous moniker, but one more authentic to the alley's true nature.

The alley's legitimate businesses serve as a smokescreen for the triad brotherhood of thieves who terrorize Cuckoo Meadows' criminal underground. After a succession of violent coups, political marriages between warring families, and Bloodstone's obliteration of hated rivals, the Gong Bao Chicken Gang has usurped the throne and has become the dominating brotherhood of thieves. Any fool who dares to snoop around their turf, asking unhealthy questions, has their end delivered swiftly at the meat grinder and the corroding stomach acids of their bloodhounds. Civilized folk and even authorities alike fear the "Jacking Chickens," save for Bloodstone, the one man all criminals loathe with shrewd fear.

Bloodstone and Miss Sierra reach Huan Wu's Gun Pow Chicken, and Miss Sierra's wristwatch reads 9:15 p.m.—she has since reset it to the proper time. The restaurant's normal hours of operation are between 9 a.m. and 9 p.m. The doors are shut, but the lights inside remain on, and dancing shadows give a sign of a couple of dozen hoodlums prattling incoherently among themselves.

"Alright, Miss Sierra, we are finally here." Bloodstone stops abruptly at the restaurant's front steps. He jets out a thin contrail of hot smoke from his recently lit cigar, nostrils flared like those of a snarling, rabid dog. His eyes narrow to daggers, and he examines the laughing and spiting shadows with calamitous intentions.

"You won't believe how many times I've eaten here since I've arrived in the city. I mean, it has it all. Good food, good ambiance, and great service, even an online five-star rating. It makes it kind of hard to imagine that management is some sort of clandestine, murderous brotherhood of thieves." Miss Sierra said with a bit of shame. "I mean, you never think your chef, the one who preps your meals with a delicate and artistic hand, could easily snap your neck or gut you like a fish all the same. I've always left generous tips for the waitresses too. I even asked my dad to wire me some extra cash just so I can dine here more often. All that trouble to fund some murderous, thieving cult's, well, thieving habits. I must say Mister Bloodstone. I can't help but paint myself a fool."

"There's no need to speak bosh things, Miss Sierra. I often dine here myself. Once a month, to be exact." Bloodstone said with clenched teeth. He holds the cigar in his mouth so he can crack his knuckles. He makes his eagerness to deliver righteous retribution upon those who have offended him more than readable. "And worry not about having unknowingly funded their illicit enterprises. A few decades back, I established an unwritten truce with the crime syndicates who infest my city—whatever profits their legitimate fronts accumulate, half must be donated back to the city with affected grins. Should they ever fail to do so, my Pulque Bunnies will be quick to report such a fatal remiss back to me."

"They're murderous thieves. I doubt they can be trusted to keep their promises. How do you know they won't try to kill you instead? If such a miracle is possible, that is." Miss Sierra asks. It has just dawned on her that Bloodstone has been parading around the city with no bodyguards or protection of any sort. *Should that worry me?*—she ponders tardily.

"What makes you think they haven't tried?" Bloodstone retorts with a hardened gaze. "They tried to poison me once. Obviously, I did not die. The poison only ended up giving me a severe case of diarrhea. Then, they tried to blow me up with a car bomb. Nothing was accomplished except for a toddler's tantrum from me after losing a fine silk suit. I was most displeased. Not to mention the utter shame I had to tolerate, strutting five blocks down, back to my penthouse with my masculinity yo-yoing about for everyone to see. And when traditional methods of murder failed, they sent some monstrous mutations after me. In the end, I had a pair of newly polished skulls mounted over my private vault's hearth. Just another conversation piece for one of my lavish late-night dinner parties."

"Sounds like they wanted to test the sincerity of your professed immortality." Miss Sierra said with a certain ghoulish shame.

"I suppose that's possible, but in all truthfulness, Miss Sierra, I'm more of a quasi-immortal. Not easily killed through conventional means, but not entirely deathless." Bloodstone said. "Pluck me with bullets, and I shall bleed. Love me, then leave me, and my heart shall break. Feather my toes, and I shall giggle. Quasi-Immortal I may be, Miss Sierra, but a mere man I still am."

"A rare breed of man you are, Mister Bloodstone. That of an extinct race of noble savages, albeit harder to kill, apparently." Miss Sierra has never heard about any such attempts on the Masked Philanthropist's life, but she dares not dispute it. Not after her traumatic experience with Macario's gifted talents. To have witnessed the fantastical invade the banality of normalcy has reawakened a forgotten sensation in her. A childlike thrill for adventure that crackles all around her soul. "Well, here we are," she turns to face Huan Wu's Gun Pow Chicken's locked doors, "just a door away from the culprits who stole your treasured box. By my count, there appear to be over a dozen thugs in there. Do you have a plan of action, Mister Bloodstone?"

"But of course, Miss Sierra. You don't get to my age surviving purely on spontaneity." Bloodstone chuckles while nostrils and teeth fume with grey smoke. He throws the stubbed cigar, stomps it with his biker boots, and gives Miss Sierra a mischievous smirk. She becomes more unsettled once he winks at her. The Masked Philanthropist turns and, with a powerful kick from his steel-clad boots, he splinters the fine mahogany door. He rushes in and growls to the unsuspecting band of thieves. "All right, you, horde of sniveling, cretinous sons of whores, ready or not, Bloodstone is here to reclaim what is rightfully his! What say you, maggots?!"

And before Miss Sierra can blink, a dreadful menagerie of pistols, revolvers, semi-automatic shotguns, and a couple of Tommy Guns, all cock in a singular rhythmic cylinder swoosh. Every barrel eyes them both with malicious intent.

"This insanity is your plan?!" Miss Sierra gulps. "Well, this is just splendid, Mister Bloodstone. As you can see now, we're surrounded by hostile goons with a rattling itch to plug us both with innumerable rounds of lead. I hope you're pleased now. Unlike you, my mortality is far more fragile."

"Lower your arms, gentlemen! If any of you fire a single shot and harm Miss Sierra, I will personally see to it that you feast upon your beating, bloodied heart. Those of you who know me well know I make no idle threats, but oaths true to my word and bonding as my blood." Bloodstone barks to the alarmed covenant of thieves. Behind the phalanx of firearms, underneath the snarls and icy glares of murder, legitimate fear seeps through the brow of every goon. Fear reflected off a single droplet of sweat. The Masked Philanthropist, though unarmed and hilariously outnumbered, dominates the situation through reputation alone.

"Plus, it'd be a shame if something bad were to happen to my nice, new jacket."—he adds cockily.

"Ha! Be thankful I find you most amusing, Masked Freak." A slim, flaky Asiatic man speaks. The man lowers his Tommy Gun and approaches Bloodstone, unafraid he taunts such a behemoth of a man. "If not, you and your lady friend here would've been riddled with bullets by now. I, Shen Yan, am the law here, and you do not frighten me Bloodstone, never have, and you're daffy to think you have any kind of power or say here. Plus, we've made our bi-monthly tribute to Cuckoo Meadows as begrudgingly agreed upon by our cunting forefathers. So, you have no reason to be busting up on our doorsteps and making baseless accusations."

"I beg to differ, my dear Shen Yan." Bloodstone coldly addresses the cocky man. "You know why I'm here, but should you stubbornly choose to continue with this ill-advised charade of insincere innocence, then let me summarize that which you know already. A week ago, a small cadre of sticky-fingered hoodlums had the *cojones* to break into my penthouse and pilfer a prized little black box from my coveted vault, just as I was away on business. Such a blatant offense against my person shan't go unpunished, nor will I leave here without my box. I strongly advise you to cut the bullshit Shen Yan and come clean with the truth before I start snapping necks and backs like dried up twigs."

Bloodstone strides coolly towards a table, grabs a pair of wooden chopsticks, and begins to toy with the wooden utensils, twirling them between his fingers. Miss Sierra keeps a careful eye on him, uncertain if she is included in the Masked Philanthropist's game or is expected to play mere spectator to his spectacularly brazen bravado. Not a wink nor a coded whisper is passed, and she has no choice but to retain a silent vigil.

"I know of what you speak. News of the theft passed through our door seconds after it occurred. We thieves are gossipers to a fault, after all. It is in our nature. But I assure you my brotherhood had nothing to do with it." Shen Yan retorts Bloodstone's accusation with a silky tone, and even Miss Sierra is unable to read through the bugger's buttery lies. "Believe it or not, Bloodstone, we are all honorable thieves here. We wouldn't dare betray the truce you've made with our forefathers. To do so would be asinine and bring forth great dishonor upon our merry crew of thieves, not to mention it'd be unwise and injurious to disrespect your slumbering savagery. Perhaps it was one of the other two brotherhoods who breached the truce and robbed you of your precious little box."

"Watch yourself, Shen Yan. I've tolerated many of your illicit enterprises in the past, at times even turned a blind eye to your far more carnivorous hobbies, so long innocents were not harmed—but to fib straight to my face and continue to do so, well, you'll quickly find yourself licking the salt off your sweaty cock."

Miss Sierra keeps herself proactive during Bloodstone and Shen Yan's verbal shootout and fiddles with her voiceless thoughts. *Did I just hear right? He turns a blind eye to the gang's more violent crimes—why Mister Bloodstone? Why would you dismiss such homicidal habits and allow them to evade justice? Do you not care? Have the centuries of quasi-eternal life stripped some of your humanity? You may not see yourself as a hero, but the entire city considers you one. You owe it to its people—to be the hero they need.*

Miss Sierra's face scrunches up with a whit of disgust towards Bloodstone. But she swiftly reconsiders such disgust, reminding herself that Bloodstone is no ordinary man.

The Masked Philanthropist has extended her the title of friend, a burdensome title that bruises hearts with tortuous emotions. Moreover, Bloodstone lauded her raw honesty and asked she remains honest and to trust him to do the same in return. Consequently, Miss Sierra decides to sheathe her sharp tongue and give Bloodstone a chance to defend his now questionable honor when the opportune moment comes.

"Threats are most unwise at your current position, Bloodstone. You are simply one man with a little girl on tow, and we are an entire flock of crazed roosters armed down to the talon and beak. We're more than ready to claw and peck your flesh in a bloodlust-fueled fray." Shen Yan backs away again, cocking his Tommy Gun at the hip. He is readably disturbed by Bloodstone's morbid oath of retribution. Past experiences have taught the conniving thief one thing—the Masked Philanthropist is above childish rhetoric like empty threats. Caution is Shen Yan's best weapon, far more reliable than the Tommy Gun at his side. "I figured you to be plain crazy before. Now I see you are plain loco instead. What idiocy makes you think we had anything to do with the theft, anyway?"

"For starters, you lack your grandfather's refined skills, Shen Yan. You see, I often allow visitors inside my vault to bask in the richness of my antique collection. I admit it's a braggadocio exhibit of my vanity. And I have but two rules for all who enter it." Bloodstone twirls the chopsticks between his fingers. He then holds them in place with a sinewy grip and claps the tips teasingly at Shen Yan. "The first rule is simple. Humor me with a pale smile and listen attentively while I recite the long-winded story anchored to each acquired object till your ears bleed with exhaustion. The second rule is just as simple. No food or drinks are permitted inside my vault. After five days sniffing every inch of my vault like a rat, I found a nibbled chicken cube and know with certainty that it came from your restaurant. My dear Shen Yan seems one of your brothers' sin of gluttony has outed you as the culprits."

"What . . .? What?! A single nibbled chicken cube? That's your proof? Your justification for bringing disrespect upon my house?—Ha! That cube could've come from any of the other 112 Chinese food restaurants in this shitty town."

Shen Yan's voice loses its silky tone. Now it is rife with nervousness.

"A clever counterargument. I applaud your efforts to mislead me, Shen Yan. But your family recipe has betrayed you. The chicken cube's saucy glaze was drizzled with a rare peanut. A peanut that is only available for purchase here at Crooks Corporate Drive. A peanut exclusive to your restaurant's famous recipe." Bloodstone points the chopsticks at Shen Yan and exclaims triumphantly, "Drop the act Shen Yan, the peanut has fingered you! Now, return what is mine before I churn your face into butter!"

"Curse that infernal peanut! You—you can't—" Shen Yan stutters madly. He turns a blood-fueled glare to a tubby man who stands to his right and spits out with scorn. "Ho Ling! You—grr—worthless fat bastard! Look at the hell your gut has brought upon us all! I knew mother should've aborted your ass."

"Sorry, Shen Yan." Ho Ling replies bashfully. "I was hungry. You should not have made me skip out on breakfast. I told you—I begged you."

"Oh, shut up. I will deal with you later." Shen Yan growls, then turns back to Bloodstone. "Seems I'm better at thieving than a battle of wits, Bloodstone. Fine, I confess, we did it. But we don't have your precious little box here. We were only hired to pull off the heist."

"The name," Bloodstone demands coldly.

"Name?" Shen Yan twists his lips with possum confusion and struts towards the Masked Philanthropist. Since he holds the client's name captive, the thief arrogantly believes Bloodstone to be in a vulnerable stance. "You expect me to disclose the name of a client? Thieves we may be, but trustworthy businessmen we are too. Our clients rely on our confidentiality and discretion, and we strive to uphold our reputation. Then again, I might make an exception if you were to just whisper a couple of Benjamins in my ear."

"The name, Shen Yan. Give—me—the name." Bloodstone repeats weighty and with monotonous tenacity. He stomps on the extortion attempt with a sledgehammer tone. "If you do, I promise not to harm you or any associate of the Gong Bao Chicken Gang. You know me to be a man of my word."

"*Crew*. It's the Gong Bao Chicken *Crew*. We've dropped the word 'gang' from our name ages ago. Huh, the word wasn't very inviting to our clients, so we changed it. PR and all that whatnot." Shen Yan corrects Bloodstone before continuing. "And I already told you, freak. I ain't telling you the client's name. Besides, you can't harm any of us. You'll be decorated with bullets if you try anything funny, and every-one here knows you strut across town without hired guns or guns of your own. So how do you propose to harm us? Eh?"

"Oh, Shen Yan. How I pity your ignorance. I'm a man of many talents, and I require no guns or bullets to cause you bodily harm, as you will learn this very second." Bloodstone chuckles with a smirk.

Suddenly, a quick blur swooshes back and forth between their grappling gazes.

Shen Yan does not quite understand what just happened. All he knows is his left eye has suddenly gone numb and dark for no appar-ent reason, and a trickling *plick, plick, plick* of red droplets follows the sudden half-blackout. A flock of shocked gasps brushes the silent air, and the entire crew of hardened thieves is agape with horror. Miss Sierra is the one person to usher a gasped, "Oh my Lord," and clasps her hands around her mouth.

Bloodstone has plucked Shen Yan's left eye

with the chopsticks. He squeezes it teasingly between the chopsticks like a moist and steamy dumpling!

"What . . .? What? Oh my," Shen Yan mumbles. The pain slowly registers in his brain, and he bellows in horror. "Oh my God! You've blinded me! Goddamn you, bastard! You took my eye! Argh, it hurts!"

"Yes . . . I can see that." Bloodstone said with sadistic sarcasm. He squishes the eyeball into mush with the chopsticks. The Masked Philanthropist shows no sympathy nor allows Shen Yan a few seconds to writhe in pain. He twirls the chopsticks playfully, shoves each stick up Shen Yan's nostrils, and lifts the thief off his feet. Bloodstone then said: "I ask again Shen Yan, the name?"

"Can't—can't give you . . . name." Shen Yan's eyes water with agony. Streams of blood flood down from his nostrils, and Bloodstone twists his grip tighter. "I . . . do that . . . and we—we're all dead . . . bastard . . . fools, shoot him down . . . Ho Ling . . . don't . . . just . . . s-s-stand there . . . f-fat . . . idiot! Shoot . . . shoot him—now!"

The meek, tubby man, Ho Ling, raises his revolver at Bloodstone with a shaky grip and stops short from the click of the trigger. He second guesses himself worried he might hit Shen Yan and is rendered stiff—the Masked Philanthropist's hardened gaze taunts him with unimaginable bruises.

"That would be most unwise, my boy." Bloodstone mocks the quivering Ho Ling. "I can easily use Shen Yan like a human shield and unwind my fury on you instead thereafter, or I can simply use the chopsticks to pluck the bullets off the air like bothersome flies and deflect them right back at you. Tell me, Ho Ling, aren't you curious to see which scenario will play out?"

"This is a tad extreme, Mister Bloodstone." Miss Sierra finally intervenes. Not for her own safety, though it is a factor, she simply refuses to remain silent and allow such brutality to continue, whether it is merited or not. Ever naïve, she still has much to learn about the *real* world. "Unhand that young man this instant, and will you please stop this moronic flirtation with Death. Not to offend you, Mister Bloodstone, but I can't imagine this object your so obsessed to reclaim is worth dying for."

"Miss Sierra, I share your sentiment. I do not wish to offend you either. Though I admire your sympathy for this pathetic excuse of a man, I advise you to be wary for whom you dispense sympathy. Sympathy in excess is both stupid and unhealthy. Think not with your heart alone, my dear, for it shatters like glass and can prove fatal." Bloodstone never turns away from Ho Ling. His voice is reasonable and courteous towards Miss Sierra. He is determined to regain his stolen black box at any cost, for reasons he alone understands. Bloodstone addresses Ho Ling again in a provocative tone. He fishes for the dark emotion caged behind Ho Ling's quivering eyes. "And we won't be dying today, am I right, Ho Ling? You are far too cowardly to fire that cannon at me. Too stupid to think for yourself. Admit it, my boy, you ain't man enough to pull the trigger. You are nothing more than Shen Yan's little bitch. My *Abuelita* was more of a man than you'll ever be!"

"Shut—shut up—I ain't anybody's bitch!" Something finally snaps inside of Ho Ling's fragile ego. Bloodstone has tugged long enough at his suppressed hatred towards Shen Yan and provokes a blind outburst. And it worked out brilliantly. Ho Ling's aim steadies, and his mouth steams with dragon breath. He barks: "I'll kill you! Die, Shen Yan!"

Three consecutive shots are fired. The bullets boom with the ferocity of thunder through the air. Miss Sierra yelps in shock, and the Masked Philanthropist's eyes glint with maligned mischief. "Beautiful," he whispers with satisfaction.

Bloodstone loosens his grip on Shen Yan. The confused thief pratfalls to the floor, and immediately proceeds to rub his bloodied nose. Among the few dozen individuals who witness what happens next, including Miss Sierra and Ho Ling, none could have ever believed such absurd feats were possible till then. But such absurd happenings are the norm in Bloodstone's world. Like a feather riding the calm winds of spring, Bloodstone's reflexes laughably defy his massive form, and he plucks each whizzing bullet from the air with the chopsticks as if they were bothersome flies. Before any eye can bat a blink, Bloodstone flicks each bullet back to Ho Ling with equal force to the revolver. One pierces his revolver hand, and one gashes his neck on the right, and another shreds Ho Ling's right ear to mush.

"My bloody ear! Ouch!" Ho Lings yelps with an agonized cry. He falls back on a pool of his own blood and a piercing ring throbs in his right ear. A series of gasps and metallic thuds follow the splashing thud. The other thieves drop their firearms, rendered too afraid to take a brave stance. Bloodstone has succeeded in establishing a firm grip of fear around their hearts. None dares to challenge his slumbering bloodlust now.

"You—you broke my nose." Shen Yan remains too focused on his own pain to care about anything else. The migraine Bloodstone bludgeoned up his nose has left him blind to everything else. "Idiots! Don't just stand there. Shoot him! He can't stop a hundred bullets all at once. You—fucking, sons of—"

Shen Yan's bark is swiftly muzzled. Bloodstone twirls the chopsticks and shoves them up his nose once again. Shen Yan's legs dangle helplessly in the air, and his eyes sweat with pained tears.

"No more fibbing Shen Yan. Your nose isn't broken. Well, not yet." Bloodstone twists the chopsticks tightly clenched to Shen Yan's nose at the nostrils. A snap and crunch are heard, and blood quickly jets out from his nostrils and washes over the wooden floors. "Now it's broken. Enough with the idle talk. Give me the name of the brave fool who ordered the heist unless you wish me to pluck out your other eye or something else far more precious. You do enjoy being a man, don't you, Shen Yan?"

"I—I . . . invoke," Shen Yan gags. Bubbles of blood gurgle from the edge of his mouth. "Invoke . . . Combat . . . Charity."—Shen Yan coughs out with a spritz of blood.

Bloodstone's eyes then quiver with disappointment.

At a loss of understanding, Miss Sierra is slightly relieved to see Bloodstone release Shen Yan from his pinched grip. Crudely, the whimpering thief sinks to the floor again. She pities the cowering Shen Yan, who caresses the soft mush that was once his nose. But her pity is not humane. It is more like pitying a sewer rat, who writhes in pain while the rodenticide it ingested through sheer stupidity slowly devours its entrails. Her pity soon becomes sickening worry when she notices Bloodstone clench his fists into sledgehammers of muscle, sinew, and bone. Combat Charity, two polar words, has transfixed the Masked Philanthropist with severe ire.

"What did you say?" Bloodstone asks with a doleful sigh.

"I invoke my right to Combat Charity, as

agreed upon by our forefathers and you at the time of the Unwritten Treaty of—of—ah, who cares." Shen Yan snarls with bloodied, clenched teeth. "Either way, you—you have to honor my request, freak. You have to!"

"Aw, shit." Bloodstone sighs disappointedly.

CHAPTER 7

AN IMMORTAL'S MERCY

Two, three generations ago, the Masked Philanthropist himself cannot quite remember the when, 'twas a dark age for Cuckoo Meadows, a new age of barbarism. At the time of Bloodstone's unexpected resurgence within the city after a century's war against the demon hordes of hell, the metropolis was besieged by the evils of human avarice. And then, after a decade of a gelded war with the Immortal Luchador, the unchallenged reign of the crime syndicates ceased abruptly, and an uneasy truce was breached with the "Masked Freak"—the fabled Unwritten Treaty.

Unwittingly, the crime lords tasted the

bitterness of surrender, but it was a better alternative to extinction. The exact reasons why an entire criminal empire abdicated its sovereign rule over the city after countless generations because of a single man has long been blemished over the decades by myth and legend. Yet one of the most infamous fairytales the old mobsters—the old surviving witnesses—would retell their children in a baptism of fear is the erasure of the Leone Crime Syndicate and their associates. The "tall tale" forewarns Bloodstone's ruthless style of justice. Apparently, the Immortal Luchador vanished them onto a hellish dimension with the aid of his Pulque Bunnies.

"Bah, rumors."—the skeptics often scoff. Yet, none has ever dared to challenge the tale's authenticity, and for generations thereafter, the exact stipulations of the Unwritten Treaty have gone mostly forgotten, except for the three most sacred ones.

Firstly, the surviving crime syndicates are to surrender half their earnings from their legitimate fronts back to the city on a bi-monthly basis. The consequences for failing to fulfill such a tribute have never been explored out of fear. Secondly, all mobsters, assassins, loan sharks, and thieving brotherhoods may go about their dirty deeds without interference from Bloodstone, so long innocents are not harmed. Lastly, there are to be no outbreaks of violence or warfare between disputing organizations for the sake of Cuckoo Meadows' citizenry and the continuing prosperity of any crime syndicate.

Thus far, none has been careless enough to surrender themselves to the damnable fires aroused by hubris. All childish scuffles—as the Masked Philanthropist refers to these petty disputes—are to be settled through the Combat Charity, a charitable close-quarter battle royal to the death between up to three warriors from each opposing party. Once a syndicate member declares Combat Charity, the other has no choice but to acquiesce to the challenge or forfeit the dispute to the opponent. The crime syndicates saw some benefit in the stipulation solely on the caveat that Bloodstone himself isn't immune to the request. Except, no one has ever dared to challenge the self-proclaimed immortal.

That is, until now and much to the Masked Philanthropist's chagrin.

The dial on Miss Sierra's wristwatch reads 10:30 p.m. An entire day has almost completely eluded them like a phantom whisper. To her, the day has been a improbable dream, a dream that is strangely touchable. She woke up at 5 a.m., and the day started out normal, same as every previous day—boring and predictable. How irrelevant it all seems now. While she slept, her dreams whisked her far away into the kaleidoscope of imagination. The world now gleams with its strange magick. But she is no longer asleep, she is now fully awake, and the magick shatters into thousands of drizzling shards. And their gleam blinds Miss Sierra with the unfettered chaos of imagination.

The day has been plagued with so many whos and whats, gun totting lunatics, Pulque Bunnies who bend and flex the very veneer of reality with a wiggle of the nose, and an entire brotherhood of jacking chickens—"what a juvenile and silly name for a band of murderous thieves," she thinks with quietude. Now, as her wristwatch ticks towards 10:35 p.m., Miss Sierra is zonked with the day's bizarreness and sits inside a derelict basement in the company of a masked quasi-immortal, who flexes and stretches every stiff muscle of his Greek-statuesque physique in preparation for a fight to the death.

Bloodstone shadow boxes under a dim light while Miss Sierra looks on silently. After Shen Yan invoked his right to Combat Charity, the Masked Philanthropist had no choice but to accept the challenge. Unsurprisingly, the quest to reclaim what is rightfully his has been elevated onto a whole new level. Now his honor has been challenged. Bloodstone himself laid down the terms of the Unwritten Treaty, and he is an honorable man to a fault. He will uphold his honor without hesitation, even if it necessitates the spillage of blood and guts. Though an immortal, the Masked Philanthropist isn't beyond basic human vices.

While Shen Yan and Ho Ling's injuries were being patched up, Bloodstone and Miss Sierra were escorted onto the restaurant's back warehouse. No foreign fingers nor batting eyes touched them, not after what Bloodstone had done to Shen Yan without shedding a single tear of remorse. They were treated with the upmost respect.

The building is much larger than what the

dining area gave away. Around fifty years ago, the structure was under the proprietorship of Corvus Technologies, a steel mill where revolutionary metals for the world android populace were molded and designed at clockwork. Once the World Government stilted the further production of "steel flesh," the structure, along with Corvus' other various steelworks factories, was liquidated. The Gong Bao Chicken Crew, as they prefer to be called now, eventually purchased the structure through a series of nonprofit organizations and charitable investors, proxies who obscure their illegitimate ventures from highly interested organizations. The front offices were sturdily refurbished, and the steel coldness of corporate power was transformed into a chic oriental dinery. And so Huan Wu's Gun Pow Chicken was born, quickly becoming a pivotal financial asset to Sugar Hill Pier and one of Cuckoo Meadows' most charitable businesses.

By day, Huan Wu's Gun Pow Chicken is the purveyor of delicious oriental cuisines while the warehouse functions as a produce receiving dock. But at the after-hours of night, the restaurant's doors shut, lock and key, and Huan Wu's Gun Pow Chicken services a different type of clientele, one seeking out gratification for a far more barbaric, even cannibalistic, hunger. The back watered warehouse smolders alight with molten fire, and the dormant steel-works engines will wake with molten liquid steel, becoming an industrial pit of hell here on Earth. An adequate gladiatorial arena for the Gong Bao Chicken Crew's illegal cage fights and Bloodstone's upcoming blood match.

"I pray you know what you're doing, Mister Bloodstone." Miss Sierra said with a cowed jitter.

They have been locked inside the decommissioned steel mill's old employee locker room for the past thirty minutes. The space is greasy, dirty, and rusted. It is hard to believe this space is technically still part of the luxurious restaurant. Every so often, Miss Sierra's heart skips a beat at the drip sounds resounding from the rusted showers, which lay a few aisles down toward the back. And the sight of creeping roaches and rats convince Miss Sierra to never dine at Huan Wu's Gun Pow Chicken ever again. From the above piping system, echoing footsteps stampede in a hurry toward the lower steel mill deck.

"Sounds like we have company. It's not just

the Chicken Crew and us anymore, is it, Mister Bloodstone?" Miss Sierra points out worriedly.

"No. Shen Yan made sure word of my fast-approaching duel spread quick to those interested in this sort of harmless vice." Bloodstone ceases punching the empty air and redirects his fists to a concrete pillar. His strength is superhuman. Miss Sierra wonders if such strength is a gift from whatever made him immortal. Bloodstone engraves his fists over the pillar's concrete. The concrete explodes to dust, and his bones do not splinter. "Little runt turned this into a prime-time brawl, no doubt in hopes to turn a profit. It does not surprise me, though. They've been having these illegal cage fights for years now. In hindsight, it makes perfect sense. Considering half their legitimate revenue unwillingly goes back to Cuckoo Meadows, they need to make ends meet somehow or else they'd lose the entire building and business."

"Why? Why do you allow this?" Miss Sierra has finally decided this is the opportune time to address the issue should Bloodstone's unlikely death come to be. "I—I heard you say something similar earlier to that Shen guy. How can you turn a blind eye to all this? I thought you wanted to help and protect the people from all ills. Turning a blind eye makes you just as complicit to sin as these thieving chickens."

"I cannot change human nature, Miss Sierra. The liberty to choose between vice and virtue is the very nature of free will. Who am I to deprive humanity of choice?" Bloodstone replies nonchalantly. He pauses his exercise and starts to unbuckle his belt. Slowly he removes his jacket and boots. "To do so will mean to abolish the human condition. What will we become then, if not something entirely inhuman? All I can do, Miss Sierra, is maintain the balance in hopes that my efforts will inspire others to be equally righteous. Do you understand me?"

"Yes. I suppose I do. Um . . . Mister Bloodstone, what are you doing?" Miss Sierra suddenly notices Bloodstone removing his jeans and white undershirt. If not for the tightly knit white loincloth, he would be completely naked. Her cheeks flush with girlish shyness. His muscular body is of godlike proportions and the first semi-nude male form she has ever seen. It is a most impressive sight.

"I'm glad you understand. Please, Miss Sierra, do not judge me so harshly because of it, and do not forget I am but one man. As for my partial nudity, I do not wish for my clothes to get torn or bloodied during the fight. It is a new outfit, and I do wish to continue modeling it for a bit longer. You don't think me vain, do you?" Bloodstone asks innocently.

"N-No. Of course not." Miss Sierra lowers her gaze. Her eyes have touched his body long enough already.

"Good. Now be so kind and help me rub this balm all around my body."

Bloodstone hands her a small metal cream jar. She cradles it on an open hand absent-mindedly. Miss Sierra looks from the tiny jar to Bloodstone's chiseled body with wide-eyed shock, finally registering what he is asking. Shyly, she blurts: "What?—What . . .?"

"Come, come now, Miss Sierra. There's no time to waste. The hour fast approaches, and Death is not a patient specter." Bloodstone barks snippily. "And I'll personally attend to my privates, so no fidgety fingers down there."

"Okeydokey," Miss Sierra replies meekly.

Miss Sierra is in awe of the Masked Philan-thropist's body, an impressive example of raw physical power. A tapestry of heroic battle scars decorates his flesh, each chronicling a past adventure.

A necklace of scars circles around his neck, Bloodstone claims it had been christened on his flesh sometime in the 1970s, during a case of a usurped body. An undead, living head had stolen his body to attain godhood. He was then forced to sport a cybernetic body, courtesy of a mad Russian scientist whose name escapes him. Months passed before he reclaimed his true body.

A monstrous visage of a feathered serpent is rippled throughout every cleft of his broad hardened back in black ink. Its crown of feathers spread triumphantly above Bloodstone's shoulders and fold down to his ribcage. If the Masked Philanthropist's tale is to be true, the Aztec god Quetzalcoatl himself etched the tattoo over his flesh back sometime during the 1960s. The Serpent God used his own blood for ink and his claws serviced as the needles. Bloodstone recalls the experience to have been quite painful.

Sometime in the 1980s, his chest was riddled with over two dozen silver bullets. Each bullet remains burrowed deep in his flesh and forms a Roman Cross pattern. The souvenir, as Bloodstone calls the vulgar memento, was a result of an attack from a mad priest who perceived his prolonged unnatural life as a blasphemous affront to God's majesty.

"Perhaps the zealot lunatic is an ancestor to our beloved Shotgun Joe. It is a possibility." Bloodstone muses aloud.

"There, that should be it." Miss Sierra finishes rubbing the mysterious balm over his calves. She hands the jar to Bloodstone and pulls it back to her chest immediately. She suddenly realizes his masked face has not been coated. "Oh, Mister Bloodstone, what about your face?"

"I'll simply rub the balm over the mask." Bloodstone grabs the jar and starts rubbing the balm all over his mask, and slightly turns away from her to attend to his privates. "Come to think about it. I cannot recall the last time I've taken the mask off. I cannot even remember what the face underneath looks like anymore. After so many years, I've grown accustomed to seeing the mask as my singular, true face."

"You've never taken the mask off?" Miss Sierra asks. "Of all the fantastical things I've seen and heard today, that one I find the hardest to believe. Doesn't it ever get hot underneath that thing? Especially wearing it all the time?"

"Not at all, my dear." Bloodstone chuckles.

"The fabric is weaved from the silk of giant man-eating silkworms from Dimension Z, I believe. The fabric responds to my body temperature and therefore only gets as hot as I do, and it's thin yet, tenacious like steel."

Loud chants echo throughout the pipes. The echoes sound something like "kill, kill" or "die, die," and the heavy drum of footsteps draw closer from down the corridor, quickly approaching. Miss Sierra's heart thunders madly. She gulps, "Guess that's the bell tolling. Do you feel ready?"

"After two hundred years, I've learned to be ready, always." Bloodstone smiles back and holds her at the shoulders. He is sympathetic to her worried heart. "I want you to know that your concern is much appreciated, Miss Sierra. I, too, find myself rather fond of you already. But you are forgetting what I have said earlier. Neither of us will die today. And I'm a man of my word."

Miss Sierra returns the eccentric Masked Philanthropist's smile with equal warmth. He is quite an empathetic man. He is right to assume she has grown fond of him in the few hours they have spent together. A rusty knob jerks, and footsteps rush towards them. It is

Ho Ling, out of breath and bandaged up. He wheezes: "We're ready for you. You should be honored. We have a full house. People came in droves when they heard you were going to be our prized brute for the night."

"Is that so? Well, I hope not to disappoint them then." Bloodstone replies. He struts past Ho Ling. "By the way, I'm glad to see you all wrapped up. No hard feelings, I hope, my dear, Ho Ling."

"No-no hard feelings. Business is business." Ho Ling said with a nervous twitch.

"Great!" Bloodstone pats him on the back, causing Ho Ling to wince with pain. "See you out there, my boy. Come, Miss Sierra. The sooner I finish this, the sooner I get back what's rightfully mine."

<hr>

Bloodstone and Miss Sierra are instructed to wait by the corridor before they are announced to the lower steel mill. The chants are much clearer now. Over a hundred people chant: "kill, kill" with bloodthirsty gusto. The steel mill had been refitted into a gladiatorial arena. A chain-link fence keeps the spectators corralled behind the bleachers, and a huge teleprompter is raised above by crude wiring ready to display the ensuing carnage with crystal clarity. The announcer's podium lays at ground level next to the gladiatorial arena. The arena itself is a large, metal platform englobed within another chain-link fence that curves into a dome and it hovers over a massive vat of orange hot, molten steel. The teleprompter fizzles on, and the makeshift stadium goes dark with pillars of light waltzing in a twirl for spectacle. And there he is, Shen Yan, on the teleprompter, sneering with glee. His nose and left eye are bandaged up good, and he still writhes with palpable hatred.

"Welcome, the unwanted scourge and undesirable outcasts of Cuckoo Meadows! The Gong Bao Chicken Crew is proud to present you with another spectacle of unbridled savagery!" Shen Yan's voice booms and the crowd goes wild with barks and howls. "Tonight, we have a most special combatant for you all! He is renowned as the weaver of fantastical tall tales! The charismatic Masked Philanthropist! Beloved by some, reviled by others! Cuckoo Meadows' favorite son! My outcast amigos and simpatico sinners, I present to you, the one and only, Bloodstone!"

Bloodstone and Miss Sierra walk down the

walkway, a mix of jubilant cheers and bitter boos erupt from the crowd. They reach the dome, and Bloodstone turns to Shen Yan, who sits at the announcer's podium a few feet to their right. "Whatever happens next, Shen Yan, I trust you'll honor the Combat Charity and keep this squabble between us gentlemen. No harm is to befall Miss Sierra. Understood?"

"I swear on my grandpappy's grave, freak. We won't harm your little dove." Shen Yan snickers.

"You better not Shen Yan. If you do, I won't hesitate to sucker punch Death square on the jaw on my way out from the nine pits of hell to beat the living shit out of you." Bloodstone's threat snatches the grin straight off Shen Yan's face. The gate opens, and the Masked Philanthropist turns to Miss Sierra one last time. "I don't suppose a good luck kiss is in order?"

"Fresh, Mister Bloodstone. Sorry to disappoint you, but that request will have to be regaled to another one of your little, tall tales." Miss Sierra teases before the gates cruelly segregate them.

Another gate clinks open from the opposite side of the arena, and two gargantuan shadows emerge in the wake of hammering footsteps.

They are twin brothers, burly elephants in the guise of men with bulging, veiny muscular bodies that dwarf Bloodstone's lean, muscular physique. The brothers engage in a short pre-battle ritual. They embrace one another in a bear hug and ram their foreheads together in a ferocious bear-like scream. They have been riled up by the fresh scent of blood and can almost savor Bloodstone's tender flesh between their snarling fangs.

"Two on one, looks like the odds are in my favor." Bloodstone cracks his neck and twirls his muscular right arm. He flexes in a braggadocio display of masculinity. "Gris and Lee, the Grizzly Brothers. I could not have asked for worthier opponents. Gentlemen, I pray you are aware our battle is a fight to the death. Consider yourselves warned. I have no intentions of holding back. Should you wish to concede me victory, now is the time."

"Huh, did you just hear what the freak said to us, Gris?" Lee, the brother clothed with alabaster white attire, chortles with roiled disbelief.

"Oi sure did, Lee." Gris, who wears all charcoal black, replies with an insulted growl. "Sounded like he wants us to surrender and turn tail. Huh, probably afraid of the hurt we are about to deliver on his Mary Sue ass."

"Yeah, yeah, took the words straight out of my mouth, Gris. Nappy ass cocksucker probably afraid to die like a man." Lee snorts back.

"I assure you, gentlemen, I fear not Death nor anyone in this plane of existence. On the contrary, I yearn for death, much like a love-lorn lad yearns for that one final, long kiss goodbye from a scorned lover." Bloodstone's eyes monitor the Grizzly Brothers. They begin to circle him like ravenous sharks lured to the scent of blood from the briny depths. "I'd only hoped to offer you mercy and spare you from the carnage I'm more than capable of inflicting. You see, I've killed a great many men in my lifetime, though never wantonly. My fists are no strangers to the warmth of blood, and my ears have gone deaf from the crackling of bone. I'm a harbinger of Death, weary of delivering death."

"You talk too much, man. Your words gonna bore me to death, yo." Gris snickers.

"This ain't a motherfucking parley freak. People are here to see you bleed and watch us crack skulls." Lee adds.

"Do you hear that, gentlemen? My heart

weeps for you both." Bloodstone cracks his knuckles, and his eyes betray his nobler personality. His spirit transforms into a hellbent beast. "Fortunately, such sentimentally was but for a pregnant pause alone. We agree, then? Regrettable, but nonetheless, to the death!"

The crowd erupts with sadistic cheer. Bloodstone rushes Gris first, and Lee rushes him from behind. Locked arm to arm with Gris, muscles grow tense, veins pulse with hot blood, and sweat trickles like droplets of rain over the steamy platform.

The fight has commenced!

Gris' strength is formidable, an almost equal match to the Masked Philanthropist's neigh superhuman strength. Almost. Locked in a deadly grip of physical prowess, both warriors' mouths jet hot breath to one another— 'tis a savage tug of war between psychological dominance and bloodthirsty will. From the corner of his eye, Bloodstone notices Lee charging him like a mad bull intent on gorging him with its horns. He cannot help but crack a smile. Though both brothers are fat with muscle, Gris is the smaller of the two and, therefore, the easiest to lift. The hulking Gris weights down on Bloodstone with the full strength of his muscular body—exactly what the Masked Philanthropist wanted him to do! Bloodstone buoys backward and manipulates the totality of Gris' strength against him. He manages to lift Gris off the floor with ease, and in a surge of impressive strength, catapults the hulking beast like a boulder straight toward his brother, Lee. The Grizzly Brothers cannonball onto each other. The force sends them both flying across the arena, and they bounce off the chain-link fence.

The crowd goes wild with laughter. It is an unforgivable humiliation for the Grizzly Brothers.

"You dare make fools out of us?!" Lee jumps back up in a fury. His pride is mercilessly singed by the crowd's salty laughter. "I'm gonna mur-derize ya cold, freak!"

"Sure, you will." Bloodstone teases and dares Lee to charge again with a wave of the hand.

There is no elegance to their fight, simply unbridled barbarism. Lee and Bloodstone exchange tightly knit and stone-clenched fisted blows in a mad blitz. Each blow tenderizes muscle and ruptures the air with sonic booms. Lee then sandwich-slams his massive palms over Bloodstone's head. The ringing, seismic waves inflict Bloodstone with momentary vertigo and cause him to drop his guard.

"I'm gonna crack ya open like the nut you are, freak!" Lee proclaims. He wraps his bulging arms around Bloodstone and locks him in a deadly bear hug.

"You—You've given me quite the headache, Lee. Kudos." Bloodstone grunts back with slight agony. "Allow me to return the favor."

Bloodstone headbutts Lee and breaks the giant's nose. Blood splatters everywhere and some of it blinds Lee. The Masked Philanthropist takes advantage of the situation and leaps into the air, spins like a top, and delivers a depth-charged duke down on the woozy Lee. The blow knocks Lee down over the bloodied floor with a loud, cracking boom. One brother is down for the count, still breathing, while the other, Gris, finally rises back to his two feet.

"Whatcha do to Lee?! Bastard, you killed him!" Gris exclaims with erroneous grief, "Brother, I'll avenge you!"

"There's no need to avenge your brother, Gris. He still draws breath." Bloodstone reaffirms Gris with reserved sympathy. "One last time, I offer you the chance to withdraw from this fight. There's no need for either of you to die here today."

"Rot in hell, Masked Freak!" Gris growls defiantly and rushes the Masked Philanthropist with an overarching clenched fist.

"Roshambo it is then, Gris. Let us find out whose rock is strongest." Bloodstone winds his right arm backward and pierces the empty air with his white-knuckled fist.

Both their fists impact together, and Bloodstone emerges the victor. The force of the Masked Philanthropist's blow ripples throughout Gris' entire arm, shredding sinew, muscle, and bone in an explosion of blood and flesh. Gris lets off a horrified and pained cry. Bloodstone's face remains stolid and cold.

"Forgive me, Gris," Bloodstone said coolly. "But as you recall, this is a fight to the death, and I did offer you fair mercy, twice. Know that you've won my respect at the very least. You and your brother have guts, but guts alone won't conquer my will to win."

With two powerful jabs to the gut, Bloodstone punctures Gris' abs and gut with his bare fists. Gris' eyes bulge with horror. The giant watches his entrails ooze out from his gaping gut and splatter over the arena grounds in disbelief.

"Oi, I got a tummy ache now. Shit . . ." He whimpers and slumps down dead.

The crowd starts to cheer the Masked Philanthropist's name immediately after the death blow. "Bloodstone, Bloodstone," they yell out. But none of their perverse praises matter to Bloodstone. The Masked Philanthropist surveys the crowd, and hunts for Miss Sierra. She is right where he left her, near the announcer's podium, and her eyes are cemented on the arena and Bloodstone himself. The cheering crowd goes silent and it vanishes from sight, and they remain alone, Bloodstone and Miss Sierra, isolated in a blank realm of their own imagining. He nods to her, and she returns the nod. A quiet understanding binds them further, both budding friends. It is a strange sensation Miss Sierra is unable to fully understand.

A rootless eeriness shakes her. The violence, the carnage, nor the deplorable disregard for civility and human decency, none of it unsettles Miss Sierra. It transfixes her with worry. All the horrible sights are new to her sheltered soul, yet she finds herself not a stranger to such macabre things. The empty feeling frightens her to the white of her bones. She becomes a stranger unto herself, and for the first time in her life, Miss Sierra questions the very nature of her character.

Miss Sierra diverts her attention to Shen Yan. He has become visibly drenched with worry after witnessing the Masked Philanthropist slaughter his first champion with ease. "Fuck me. This—this can't be happening."—he mouths. Miss Sierra notices his right palm hover over a red button while his single right eye divides its attention between the button and the fight. *What are you planning to do with that button, Shen Yan?*—Miss Sierra questions before returning her attention to the arena.

Lee's vision is spotty with polka-dots of white light. Nonetheless, he recognizes his brother Gris sag over the battlefield, dead, next to the wet mush that is his guts. His fists hammer and dent the arena's metal platform. "Griiiiiis! Nooo!"—he howls madly, and giant pink beads of sweat, blood, and tears trickle down his face.

The Masked Philanthropist knows Lee's lamentation will be temporary before he seeks out demonic retribution upon him. He does not waste a single minute and acts quickly.

Without hesitation or a flinch of disgust, he goes arm deep inside Gris' discarded, bloodied organs.

During his youth, sometime in the 1950s, Bloodstone worked at the local butcher shop in the small, impoverished pueblo where he grew up. The job often required him to sort out the bloodied intestines, livers, and hearts of the freshly gored pigs. This current act is no different to him. Bloodstone's centuries-long conflict with mankind's sinful aspects has convinced him they are pompous creatures incapable of forgoing their appetite for destruction, much like any other animal. He sorts through the organic mush and pulls out the intestines. He then hastily ties it into a knot and creates a soft and wet lasso with a noose.

Confused and drunk with hatred, Lee rushes toward the Masked Philanthropist, intent on avenging his fallen brother. Bloodstone's moves are far more graceful and tactful, as opposed to Lee's more savage attack. Bloodstone bends at the knees and takes a backward leap. Midway through his aerial somersault, when he hovers over Lee's massive form, Bloodstone ensnares his neck with the gutty noose. "What the hell?"—Lee mumbles, a ticking second before

Bloodstone pulls him down from the neck with the organic rope. Lee falls to his side, and the Masked Philanthropist rushes him, wasting no time to lasso him into submission.

Immobile and at the mercy of Bloodstone, the noose tightens around Lee's neck and slowly denies him fresh breaths. Everything starts to go dark around him, and Lee hears Bloodstone's faint echo. "Submit, Lee, and concede my victory. You don't have to join your brother in death."

Lee flaps his wrist like a frantic, caged bird and declares defeat. Bloodstone has won the battle in a mere fifty seconds, shy ten from a whole minute—a new record. The crowd erupts with glee, chanting the Masked Philanthropist's name with pride. Except for Shen Yan, whose single right eye quivers with disbelief and dread.

Bloodstone loosens the noose off Lee and allows him to repose in his slumbering exhaustion. Miss Sierra sighs with relief. She cradles Bloodstone's clothing in her arms and strides to the announcer's podium. "It's over Shen Yan. Mister Bloodstone won your sick game. Now honor your end of the bargain and release him."

"N-no, this . . . this isn't fair." Shen Yan mutters bitterly.

"The name, Shen Yan. As we agreed, give me the name of the one who ordered the heist." Bloodstone yells from across the arena triumphantly. He sits atop the unconscious Lee to further punctuate his victory. "In accordance with the Combat Charity and as agreed upon by your forefathers, you have no choice but to honor my request."

"Fuck the forefathers! They were dickless old farts for ever having feared a mere man. For all we know, you ain't immortal or even the same person who forced the treaty down our throats! And while we're on the subject of fuckwads—fuck you too!" Shen Yan yells back defiantly. He smiles sinisterly and then presses the very same red button his palm hovered over throughout the entire fight.

The steel mill's entire foundation begins to quake from the clockwork grind of subterranean gears. To Miss Sierra's terror, the gladiatorial arena's metal platform creeks open, plummeting Bloodstone and the unconscious Lee to the revealed underneath pool of molten steel. Yet, strangely, Miss Sierra swears the

Masked Philanthropist cracked one final smirk and shared a rather mischievous wink with her.

Splash, splash. Bloodstone and Lee melt away in the pool of molten steel.

Shen Yan jumps off the podium, high off the dastardly kill. The unanimous boos that welcome his descent bother him none. Miss Sierra rushes him and slugs him across his one remaining good eye. She reprimands him with a drenched breath. "You son of a bitch! You gave him your word! Have you no shame?!"

"Quiet woman, or you'll burn next!" Shen Yan strikes her across with an open hand. Miss Sierra is sent flying back, eyes thick with streams of tears. She looks at Shen Yan with shock.

The treacherous thief shamelessly boasts his cowardly victory aloud and with a freshly bruised eye. "I did it! I've killed the Masked Freak! Ha-ha-ha! Sorry to disappoint you, dear readers, but *Metropolitan Mexploitation* has come to an abrupt and mediocre conclusion!"

Suddenly, a quaking hammer from below the surface, perhaps somewhere nearby the sewers, sends a second seismic wave across the steel mill. The relentless hammer of fists over concrete effectively shushes Shen Yan's premature gloats. The quaking hammer comes in pairs every second, and the pounding fists dig themselves upward onto the surface. *Boom, Boom*—another chorus echoes.

"Not possible," Shen Yan whimpers.

Then, hot steam hisses out from the service pipes and ventilation system. The spectators become spooked and stampede out in throngs. They tumble and stomp over each other like spurred wildebeest. Then follows the familiar voice that echoes with utter conceit.

"Oh, is that so Shen Yan? That's not what our most respectable author has promised me." It is Bloodstone, alive and well. "I was promised prose of epic proportions, chronicling my most bizarre adventures yet. And I promised him dictated soliloquies waxing my 101 years of self-inflicted damnation leading up to the present day. From my baptism into immortality to my odyssey across the oceans of imagination, there are still many stories for our starving author to scribe. My dear, Shen Yan, you'll find that *Metropolitan Mexploitation* still has many adventures to exploit."

A singular fist pierces through the concrete floor, followed by another and another until a large gaping hole has been dug from underneath. Hot steam jets out, and the Masked Philanthropist lunges out. He lands on all fours over the floor, back arched, before Miss Sierra and a quivering Shen Yan. Steam fumes from every minuscule orifice of his skin, yet the Masked Philanthropist's body is naked of melted flesh and smoky blisters and gleams like a glazed ham.

"Mister Bloodstone, you—you're alive!" Miss Sierra exclaims with relief. She dashes to his side. "But how?"

"Not too close, Miss Sierra. I'm fresh out of the oven, sort of speak, and the hot steam will surely scald you." Bloodstone halts her short from his smoking, blazing body. "Thanks only to the balm that I'm still alive. The oily substance is an organic extract harvested from the mucus-secreting warts of extra-dimensional, bull-sized, cannabis-smoking Mammoth Toads. Its otherworldly properties protected me from the molten steel's liquefying heat. I had anticipated Shen Yan's betrayal from the start. That's the thing about cowards. They're irritably predictable. Obviously, poor Lee didn't make it. Pity. Now, Shen Yan, I believe you and I have some business to conclude."

"This—this is a nightmare." Shen Yan

babbles like a tot. "You can't be alive. Oh God, what tortures is that twisted brain of yours conjuring? What horrors are you planning to do to me?"

"Miss Sierra, would you please toss me a cigar from my jacket." Miss Sierra obeys Bloodstone's request and tosses him a cigar. The Masked Philanthropist grabs it and presses the butt up against one of the fizzling bullets drilled into his chest to light it. He then takes a good drag. "Depends on how I gauge the many insults you've spat at me. Let us weigh down the list, shall we, Shen Yan. First, you've betrayed the sacred principles of the Combat Charity, which you yourself erected. Then, you attempted to murder me after I defeated your champions. Lastly, you had the audacity to break the fourth wall and, worse of all; you harmed Miss Sierra! For these insults, I shall never forgive you, Shen Yan!"

"Please! Oh please, don't kill me!" Shen Yan drops to the floor and grovels for his life. He curls up like a disgusting pill-bug next to Bloodstone's bare feet. "I—I will give you what you want—Chupacabra! El Chupacabra was the one. He is who ordered the heist. He—he's cradled up at Copperhead Dock, Dock 18B, building 412. Just please, please don't kill me!"

"Chupacabra . . . I should have known. Thank you, Shen Yan. You have been most helpful. Still," Bloodstone grabs Shen Yan's collar and pulls him in close.

"Wait, what are you doing? I gave you the name you—" Shen Yan snivels.

But Bloodstone's heavy palm slaps the thief's cowardly pleas twice. A few teeth are knocked out, as well.

"That's for dishonoring the Combat Charity, plus the added attempt on my life. And this . . ." Bloodstone then plucks Shen Yan's remaining right eye with his bare fingers, brutally blinding him. ". . . is for harming Miss Sierra."

"Argh! I've been blinded!" Shen Yan shrieks. Bloodstone drops him to the floor and leaves him to writhe in agony.

"Yes . . . I can see that." Bloodstone flips the eyeball to the floor and stomps it like a grape with his bare foot. "We'll be seeing each other around, Shen Yan. Come, Miss Sierra, 'tis time for us to bring this adventure to its natural end."

Miss Sierra follows behind the Masked Philanthropist. She takes one brief look back to the writhing Shen Yan. She finally understands what Bloodstone meant about tempering one's sympathy. Though a noble gesture, too often, vermin like Shen Yan exploit it. Bloodstone is without sympathy for the parasites who leech off the vices of humanity, but at the very least, he is merciful.

CHAPTER 8

EL CHUPACABRA

"**M**ister Bloodstone, you're bleeding." Miss Sierra is overwhelmed with sincere surprise seeing the Masked Philanthropist bleed. After witnessing him survive a dip in a pool of hot molten steel, she did not believe him vulnerable to mortal weaknesses, not even Death's indiscriminate touch. Yet, true as rain, Bloodstone coughs out blots of blood over a white handkerchief. His own blood. "Silly sot, you're probably bleeding internally. We have to get you to a hospital immediately."

"Hm?" Bloodstone is unbothered with Miss Sierra's diagnosis. Unaccustomed to such matronly concern, Bloodstone blushes underneath the mask and tucks away the bloodied handkerchief back inside his jacket—having fully clothed at this point—in a jitter. "I'm quite alright, Miss Sierra, nothing to get alarmed about. My body is merely bruised, not torn. Bleeding is a minor consequence of battle, and undying battle is the downside of immortality as is pain. Fortunately, I've made it a habit to always carry around painkillers in the eventuality of any unforeseen or unavoidable bouts of battle."

Bloodstone pulls out a medical capsule from his jacket and pops out three pills. He ignores Miss Sierra's agape expression and flicks the pills inside his mouth, and swallows.

"So . . . you do feel pain?" Miss Sierra sighs sharply in disbelief. First, he bleeds, and now Bloodstone confess to feeling pain. After everything she has witnessed throughout this crazy and noisy day, it is becoming more difficult for her to perceive that Bloodstone, a paragon of evolutionary perfection, can be hurt. "I have many doubts, Mister Bloodstone, and the opulence of immortality is among them now. How . . . how long have you been fighting?"

"A very long time, Miss Sierra. It may be a bit of an exaggeration, but I believe I might've burst forth from my mother's womb fully grown, fully ready for an eternity of battle." Bloodstone replies somberly.

"I remember reading about you in my father's newspaper, and hearing the other children recite your tall tales in the playground as a child. Your tall tales always filled me with wonder, and they were my escape from my inland island." Miss Sierra said timidly. She fidgets her fingers together as she usually does whenever excited or nervous. "Anyway, my father eventually learned about my growing fascination for adventure and Cuckoo Meadows . . . he strongly disapproved of this odd behavior of mine. I guess, he never quite accepted that his own daughter was odd, too, much like you."

"I sense there's another question coming my way. There's no need for all this cushioning, just go ahead and ask away, Miss Sierra." Bloodstone said impatiently.

"Shotgun Joe and the Grizzly Brothers, both enemies you conquered or slain with brutal efficiency, and let's not forget how you permanently deprived Shen Yan of sight." Miss Sierra pauses to take a short breath, then continues. "Mister Bloodstone don't misunderstand me here. I don't fully condemn you for matters beyond my grasp of understanding, but I cannot stop questioning if perhaps you revel in all this violence. Well, do you?"

"A bold and misguided question, Miss Sierra. No, I find little pleasure in this inescapable wheel of violence, torture, and death. You claim to be an odd creature like myself, then perhaps you can understand what I'm about to say. Unlike you, escape from my island of immortality is nigh impossible. Allow me to elaborate. A great many faces have come and gone in my two odd centuries of unnatural life. Some were loved, while others hated, yet both with equal passion. A pity. I can't seem to recall most of those faces . . . even their names elude me now." Bloodstone's voice unwinds from its usual bravado and soothes to a gentler, more vulnerable timbre. "Immortality . . . is a strange kind of cruelness, to say the least. Though the spiraling years temper your fears, they, too, sinisterly rob you of your most precious memories. Immortality has taken much from me, Miss Sierra, when I've sacrificed so little in return. Yet, I am blest to still feel pain. You see, the pain, however small, gives me a taste of the bittersweet promise of death. A death I hunger, a death I may never savor. Immortality has taught me it is better to fade with your memories rather than yearn to relieve them for all eternity."

"But you said you were more of a quasi-immortal, a mere man although one difficult to kill." Miss Sierra sees a different aspect of the Masked Philanthropist. He is many things to different people. An astute businessman to a stock market enthusiast, a folkloric icon to the common folk, and a murderous beast of retribution to the criminal element. But Miss Sierra sees a mere man anchored to a great fear of eternal aloneness, a life without end or memory. "This may be a strange thing for me say, but I'm thinking you might've lied to me earlier in the day. Nothing on this world can truly kill you."

"You are mistaken again, Miss Sierra." Bloodstone chuckles. Miss Sierra isn't so much in the humorous mood and remains silent. "I've never lied to you, not then or now, and I've no desire to dishonor or corrupt our budding friendship with lies or half-truths. I might lean slightly on a higher, preternatural plateau than most people, but I promise you, I am still nothing more than a mere man."

"I must be going crazy when I'm unable to believe the sanest thing I've heard all day." Miss Sierra said with a wryly laugh. "You're no mere man, Mister Bloodstone. But you're quite the charming enigma. If you are a mere man as you're so stubbornly claiming, then what can kill you?"

"With that type of inquiry, I might think you to be an enemy spy sent to burrow and expose my darkest secrets." Bloodstone laughs. "No, Miss Sierra, you're no spy, that I am certain. I trust you to a degree, but we've many more adventures to share before we reach that threshold of trust."

"Why Mister Bloodstone, I think you've grown a bit today." Miss Sierra teases. "You're much wiser with whom you trust."

"Wiser, I am. This week's betrayal was a hurtful reminder that it's not our enemies we must watch closely, but our friends. For it is only those closest to our hearts who can cause us the greatest of harm." Bloodstone's thoughts suddenly set him adrift in his centuries' long past. He becomes lost in a plane of eternal aloneness, light-years away from Miss Sierra, and still, he calls out to her. "You know, since the dawn of time, when the world was much smaller, and our existence more delicate, mankind warred endlessly against itself in the name of duty, honor, and loyalty to God and country. Yet all the conquests and holocausts they unfurled upon themselves were desperate, destructive attempts to attain . . . immortality. What fools were they, for I know what true immortality is—a broken and contrite existence."

"Mister Bloodstone, are you all right?" Miss Sierra asks. The sound of her tender voice breaks the Masked Philanthropist's trance.

"Hm?" Bloodstone, visibly shaken, shrugs off whatever thoughts clouded his focus. "Forgive me, Miss Sierra, think nothing about what I've just said. Ofttimes, I tend to prattle on nonsense. It's no surprise then, why certain people think me . . . unhinged. Though none are brave enough to say it to my face. A minor hiccup, I assure you. Quickly now, Miss Sierra, the dock is a mere few blocks past Umiko Rompopo's Aquarium. Let us bring today's adventure to an end."

Copperhead Dock, the massive 850-acre warehouse district of seedy, derelict buildings, lies southwest of Sugar Hill Pier's harbor. The architecture's cold, industrial design is a dark polarity to Sugar Hill Pier's other warmer, artistically vibrant districts. While the rest of the borough inspires vitality and brims with the celebrated joys life has to offer, Copperhead Dock is an ugly satire of that same vision. Miss Sierra has never seen a more grotesque personification of Death than the rotting architecture at Copperhead Dock.

Dock 18B is the outermost dock, and Building 412 borders the coastline, fated to constantly endure the soft push of the cascading ocean waves. Miss Sierra's wristwatch ticks at 11:45 p.m., midnight fast approaches, and they lay hidden behind Building 411. Building 412, a five-story storage facility, lies around the corner. This time around, the Masked Philanthropist is less impulsive and more cautious about whatever dangers might await them.

Bloodstone peeks from behind Building 411 and examines the front entrance of Building 412 with a falcon's eye. There are no guards nor security cameras, and no sounds are heard, except for the soft electrical hum of the lantern posts and the soothing crash of the waves against the dock. The inconspicuous atmosphere confirms Bloodstone's suspicions—their villainous host is expecting them. There is no doubt, Shen Yan warned El Chupacabra about Bloodstone and Miss Sierra's arrival, justly spiteful after Bloodstone permanently robbed him of sight.

Bloodstone and El Chupacabra have met but once before, some three years ago, at a charity event hosted by Julius Tiberius Nero III, a prestigious and well-respected Judicial Officer of the World Court. The honorable Julius introduced both men, and they took an immediate disliking to one another.

El Chupacabra was a youngblood gangster at the time. He snarled with an insatiable hunger to not only make his bones but to devour them as well. His ruthlessness and machete-sharp cunning allocated him the undisputed crown of Cuckoo Meadows' underworld enterprises. In a short span of five years, every criminal syndicate pledged loyalty to El Chupacabra. Those who opposed his rule paid the price in blood. Rumors of his cannibalistic taste reached a legendary status that rivaled Bloodstone's reputation as an undying, creative storyteller. The stories whispered among mobsters, and their goons speak about El Chupacabra's fearsomeness true to his namesake. They say he dries out his enemies' veins to suckle on their fresh blood whilst he feasts upon their hearts.

If the tales told are to be true, El Chupacabra

prefers his hearts medium rare and bathed moist in tabasco sauce.

Over the five years the "Silent War" raged on, the criminal element's flirtation with savagery nearly led to its utter, mutual annihilation. Nothing would have pleased the Masked Philanthropist more than to see the pestilence of crime implode on itself. For the great majority of the war, Bloodstone avoided direct interference, so long the three sacred laws of his treaty were not violated. And for the first two and a half years of the Silent War, the greater populace of Cuckoo Meadows went about their unimportant lives utterly ignorant to the carnage stirring right underneath their trotting feet. But peace, unlike Bloodstone, is not entirely immortal, and it wasn't long before the violence of war infected civility and harmony. Mauled, dismembered corpses, along with the usual severed head, started to be discovered across Cuckoo Meadows.

A frozen goods truck arrived at Cooks Corpus Drive one early morning. In its invoice, the driver expected to make the routine delivery of meats and fish, poultry, produce, and dairy. Regrettably, nowhere in the invoice was there mention of the five frozen, dead bodies crammed among its inventory, each hanged on hooks through the jugular.

The driver claimed not to know where the bodies came from.

Two weeks later, Cuckoo Meadows' Water and Power Department received a call from Midtown's Xochitl Luxury Suites. Tenants and management complained about the hotel's constipated water pressure, which cut off water service to their higher level—and more lucra-tive—suites. The service tech sent to remedy the issue nearly spat out his own guts when he discovered over twenty shriveled and noisome corpses jammed snuggly into the hotel's main service pipeline. A few hours later, at a Dirty Southsville neighborhood playground, twelve severed heads on pikes traumatized the seven children who unsuspectingly went in to enjoy the sands, swings, and ballcourts with their frozen, agonized faces.

The defiling of the youth's innocence was the final straw for the Masked Philanthropist.

While other mobsters kept their savagery under the yoke of humility, and away from the Masked Philanthropist's ever prying eyes, El Chupacabra—spurned by his own hubris— was far too eager to prick Cuckoo Meadows' rosy pulse with a lethal injection of fear and terror. The capriciousness of youth was El Chupacabra's greatest sin and it served to earn him Bloodstone's immediate loathing.

When first introduced at Julius' charity event, the Masked Philanthropist made sure to leave an everlasting impression with the pompous El Chupacabra.

"So, you're the one I've heard so much about. The bane of Cuckoo Meadows' underground enterprises." El Chupacabra hissed with a deep, throaty voice. "You don't look like much, boy. And frankly, I don't see what all the fuzz is about."

"Ditto. Words can't express how much I've looked forward to our meeting." Bloodstone locked hands with El Chupacabra, ready for a gentlemanly shake. "Ergo, I shall let my actions do the speaking for me instead."

Then, El Chupacabra's howling cries shortly followed the recognizable sounds of bone going snap, crackle, and pop. The Masked Philanthropist had broken El Chupacabra's right arm in five different places. El Chupacabra's entourage was quick to escort him out thereafter in a trail of tears. El Chupacabra had been served cold humiliation, courtesy of Bloodstone.

"This town will be my whore one way or another! I'll show them all that you're no god, just a man!" El Chupacabra barked back to the Masked Philanthropist. "And no man is beyond my control, not even you. I will own and brand your ass with my cock, you Masked Freak! You hear me?! You'll pay for what you've done to me!"

The Masked Philanthropist paid him no attention. He occupied himself casually brushing lint off his blazer and resumed to enjoy the remainder of the night with a nice glass of red wine.

Shortly thereafter, Cuckoo Meadows was freed from the plague of macabre sights.

El Chupacabra's threats echo in Bloodstone's head while he scribbles a short annotation over a small, rolled-up piece of paper. Bloodstone then lights it with his silver Zippo lighter, and the parchment slowly fizzles out in green flames.

"I'm quite tired of asking so many questions," Miss Sierra sighs wearily. "But I've got ask either way, what was that business all about?"

"Just a quick string of instructions for my Pulque Bunnies," Bloodstone replies. "Things are about to move quickly now, Miss Sierra. I advise you stretch your legs just about now."

"First thing I do every morning, Mister Bloodstone." Miss Sierra creeps under the Masked Philanthropist's towering physique and joins in on the peeking. "Strange, I don't see any guards at the door. Maybe Shen Yan lied about the location to give his master a running chance."

"Not likely. Shen Yan knows better by now, and I'm confident he has no desire to see the consequences for trying to deceive me." Bloodstone notices that Miss Sierra cocks him a brow. The Masked Philanthropist bashfully rubs the back of his neck. He has forgotten about the punishment he had enforced upon Shen Yan earlier. "I meant figuratively, of course. Anyway, El Chupacabra is more than aware of our unannounced visit. As we speak, he waits for us."

"Then, what are we waiting for—?" Miss Sierra's question is answered shortly after she utters the last word. A soft olive glow slowly materializes next to them.

Her skin starts to bubble with gooseflesh, and an eerie, otherworldly force pollutes the cool harbor mist. Miss Sierra gasps with the recall of trauma. The brick wall next to them ripples like a calm spring suddenly patted by a singular raindrop. A familiar strangeness crawls all about her skin. It carries the same cold, ghostly touch she felt earlier in the day when she and Bloodstone were unsuspectingly swallowed up by Macario the Pulque Bunny's Grey Warren. A figure steps out from the vertical rippling pool. Miss Sierra thought it to be Macario again, but she is mistaken. A slightly shorter, more robust individual, queer like Macario, emerges. A long, dirty green trench coat wraps the Pulque Bunny's body, and a forest thick, frizzled black beard shrouds his face while his eyes lay sheltered underneath the visor of a black cap.

"Hiya, boss. Lovely night for a stroll, is it not?" The Pulque Bunny speaks in a low, monotone whisper. Miss Sierra is barely able to hear him clearly.

"Anton, my shaggy and briny Bunny!" Bloodstone exclaims. "Good to see you again, my cloistered and quiet friend. It has been too long."

"Aye, that it has, boss. Sorry for the tardiness, boss, been busy entertaining the old gargoyle. Good news, he won't be bothering you no more. I got your note, by the way, old

Mackie boy—" Anton stops short when he spots Miss Sierra next to Bloodstone.

Anton is left mouth agape, with the bottom lip dangling in a bounce. He lifts the cap's visor to steal a proper quick peek of Miss Sierra. Anton's marble black eyes stun her with surprise before he scurries them back under the cap's visor.

The bedraggled Pulque Bunny then greets her with an extended, open hand and a low whisper. "Pl-please to make your acquaintance miss. I am Anton, and who be you?"

"Hello Anton, I'm Rubí Sierra. Nice to meet you too." Miss Sierra shakes Anton's hand. She notices him dart his gaze to the floor. He gently kicks the floor and sheepishly tugs the sleeves of his trench coat. The queer Bunny's childlike nervousness flatters her quite a bit. She smiles.

"I—I heard about you from old Mackie boy. He made no mention of what a pretty star you are." Anton said bashfully.

Anton's kind appraisal embarrasses Miss Sierra. She cannot help and brush her medium-length hair to the side.

"Yes, she is quite the moon flower in the night sky," Bloodstone interjects. "Enough of this schoolyard flirtation Anton. You said you received my note. Ergo, I'm free to assume everything with Block has been sorted out and that everything else will be in order once midnight approaches, correct?"

"Uh, um . . ." Anton mumbles with unease before answering Bloodstone. "Yeah—yeah, everything will be green by then, boss. And old Mackie boy sends a message, boss. He found Block and brought him back home. Poor Block, always a slave to his heart, and you know how much he loves you, boss. We all do. And as a testament of our deathless love, we made a hard bargain with that old, molting gargoyle—if we shall ever fail you again, we'll rescind our covenant with you, whereupon he is free to deport us back to the underworld where we will toil in the Ethereal Wheat Fields of the Restless, cultivating the Spirit Jugs of Purification under the stewardship of Mistress Nexoxcho."

"Anton . . ." Bloodstone's eyes bulge with horror. The Pulque Bunny's odd confession has him quivering at the knees. He kneels and holds Anton tightly at the shoulders. He then berates him. But the Masked Philanthropist's voice is not filled with anger but rich with fear and sorrow. "You melodramatic fools! What have the three of you done, Anton?! Tell me!"

"Boss . . . we have made peace with our failure and 'twas the only way for us to get Block back," Anton replies emptily.

"So, you have—I promise you, old friend, no matter how difficult it may be, I will amend this, this lapse in judgment," Bloodstone said with profound compassion. "For now, go get your brothers and do as I have instructed to the dot."

"Will do, boss." Anton turns back to the brick wall, dips his finger on it, and the fabric of reality ripples again. "We won't fail you again, boss. Promise we won't."

With a gruff smile across his face, Anton the Pulque Bunny melts away with the ripple.

"Mister Bloodstone . . ." Miss Sierra is at a loss to what exactly transpired between the Masked Philanthropist and the mysterious Pulque Bunny. Nonetheless, she tries her best to reach out to his aching heart.

"When I first met them, they were like frightened little birds, unwillingly, cruelly hunted to near extinction and then smuggled away from their home to a foreign land. After many years and other tribulations, they learned to accept this strange land as their new home. They, too, grew to love its people as much as they love their liquor." Bloodstone sighs and wipes droplets of tears from the corner of his eyes. "For some time now, an envoy of the underworld has been threatening to deport them back to their rightful realm. Anton and the others have always refused him before, but this entire debacle has clouded their reasoning. They have just now made a pact with this old gargoyle. Should they fail me again, they shall rescind their life debt to me and migrate back home. They aren't simply my Pulque Bunnies, Miss Sierra. They are my friends, my only friends before you, and it is I who has failed them."

Bloodstone's voice trembles with a mixture of emotions, anger, sadness, and fear commingle to create a bleak cloud of uncertainty. Miss Sierra looks up to the Masked Philanthropist with newfound respect. He weeps without shame in fear of losing his Pulque Bunnies. In fear of losing the sole family he knows.

"The clock is ticking, Miss Sierra, and time waits for no one. Come, let us not keep our villainous host waiting further." Bloodstone continues with stern resolve.

Miss Sierra says nothing in return and follows the Masked Philanthropist's impressionable footsteps, eager to finally uncover the mystery of his stolen black box. *What precious treasure could it be safeguarding?*—she wonders.

The Masked Philanthropist's fists hammer the wooden door, and from behind, worried whispers conspire among themselves. A soft, metallic swipe is heard, and from the peephole, a cyclopean eye quivers with palpable fright at the sight of Bloodstone. "You—it's you. Big boss has been expecting you," the voice from behind the door said. A sequence of fifteen locks go unlocked, and the purring creek of the door welcomes them inside. Bloodstone storms in, Miss Sierra, follows suit, though a bit more timidly. Five snarling goons salute them, each with Tommy Guns at the palms aimed straight at them. Miss Sierra rolls her eyes. She has had her fill of Death's empty promise for a lead-laced reckoning.

"Gentlemen, a good evening to you all." Bloodstone maintains a diplomatic tone, no doubt a temporary ploy until his prized box is within sight. "Forgive this late-night intrusion on whatever nefarious schemes you may be plotting for the remainder of the week, but

I'm sure you all know why my associate and I are both here tonight. Now, for lack of better words, take me to your leader."

Miss Sierra and Bloodstone are hastily escorted down a long, dark corridor. A lone goon guides them from the forefront, the remaining four trails behind with the barrels of their Tommy Guns dollying to the Masked Philanthropist's every move. Static burps cause the ceiling lights to blink at every step they take, and a dank, putrid stench invades Miss Sierra's nostrils with scathing hatred. It could be a mound of shit or a heap of rotting corpses or both, it is hard to tell the smell's feculent origin.

The goons pay Miss Sierra no reasonable attention, and she is strangely roiled. She is being treated like nothing more than a bothersome commodity, a common accessory to Bloodstone. Though Miss Sierra understands the hard truth that Bloodstone alone poses any authentic threat, she does not appreciate being treated with the slightest of indifference. But there is a harder truth here, Miss Sierra wrestles with sensations of uselessness and helplessness. Not to mention, the harpy wail of her haughty mother keeps ringing in her ears. Her insecurities have always been a vile poison that crippled her attempts to ascend onto greatness, and blinding, too. And perhaps tonight, she will outgrow her poison.

They reach the far end of the corridor and stop at a pair of double doors. Their guide cautiously knocks on the doors. While they wait for a reply, Miss Sierra manages to catch Bloodstone examining the stairway to their left with great interest. *What are you planning?*— it has just struck Miss Sierra that once again, the Masked Philanthropist has excluded her from whatever mischief is at play to reclaim his stolen box. At this point, it would be pointless to argue with him. Miss Sierra can only hope that his plan includes them escaping with their lives intact.

The day's weird happenings have certainly warped and weft like a domino effect, and she is more than ready for whatever madness awaits them from behind the double doors. Miss Sierra then snickers to herself. She has finally succumbed to the insanity that gnarls and twists the malleable world. Such a notion isn't too farfetched when considering Miss Sierra has finally learned to trust the Masked Philanthropist.

"What is it?" A gravelly voice growls from behind the doors.

"It's Pauly boss and, uh, I got the Masked Freak and his dame with me." The goon named Pauly replies with a shaky voice.

"Bloodstone's here? Well then—bring him in, you dolt!" The voice barks back.

Pauly bursts the doors open and hurriedly waves them in with his Tommy Gun. The seedy room is well lit. A long window gives view to the sparkling, icebound ocean. It is a picturesque sight, with the cool blue hue of the moon refracting off the careening waves and the small service boat patrolling the coast not too far from the building. Bloodstone smiles at the sight of the boat, much to Miss Sierra's continued bafflement. A solitary desk lays at the center, and to its far-right corner sits the Masked Philanthropist's little black box. The chair at the desk faces away from them with a man reclined on it, taking in the serene view of the ocean under the pale blue moon. The cocking Tommy Guns halts them a short foot away from the desk, away from the black box. The chair swivels round with a squeak, and El Chupacabra reveals himself.

El Chupacabra is unlike what Miss Sierra

initially imagined. He is dwarfish, obese, balding, and wears a tasteless mustard plaid suit. He is a grotesque caricature of cinematic gangsters, devoid of their silky charisma and oily good looks. El Chupacabra snarls a grin and rubs the goatee stubble decorating one of his double chins. He rises from his seat with a breathless huff and wobbles towards Bloodstone.

"Why Bloodstone, what took you so long?" El Chupacabra grins to the Masked Philanthropist, showcasing rows of sharp teeth that are less human and more shark-like.

"Chupacabra, I'll be frank with you—this day has been most taxing. I am in no mood to put up with anymore shenanigans from you or anyone else tonight. It's five till midnight, and I'm tired and hungry and rather irked that I missed my nightly sitcoms. Sure, I can always record them, but it's just not the same after." Bloodstone winks at Miss Sierra before continuing. "Look, Chupacabra, our mutual hatred notwithstanding, we are both reasonable businessmen. So, here's my proposal. Give me back what's rightfully mine, and let us both go without a scuffle, and in exchange, I won't kill you."

"Kill me?" El Chupacabra pulls his head back in a gurgling, hoarse laugh. The mobster wipes a few tears off his narrow eyes. Bloodstone's fearless candor amuses him. "You really are a special type of stupid, Masked Freak. This ain't no business transaction here. It's a show of power. I told you, no one is beyond my control. Not even you. One day, Bloodstone, one day this city will be my whore. You see, I may rule over the criminal underworld, but it's all for naught, not so long they fear you above me."

"Very well said Chupacabra, and strangely, I sympathize. What good is the crown if no one will honor you as the one true king of Cuckoo Meadows?—I simply don't understand how the theft of my most prized possession fits into all of this." Bloodstone said with a forked tongue. "If you so desired to reaffirm your rule in the eyes of your lackeys, then you should have called my office and set up an appointment with my secretary, Yasmine. That way, we could've dispensed with the pointless hindrances and had us a proper duel for the very soul of Cuckoo Meadows. You know, mano-a-mano."

"Ha! You think me a fool, Bloodstone?" El Chupacabra spits back and wags an accusatory finger to the Masked Philanthropist. "I don't swallow none of your fictitious bullshit, your so-called tall tales, or the myths surrounding your alleged immortality. But I'm a cautious man who trusts his gut instincts. It's the only way I've survived so long in this murderous game of musical chairs. I know you're not a man to be trifled with, and after what I've heard from Shen Yan, I see my instincts have been most beneficial to my wellbeing."

"Miss Sierra, would you be so kind as to tell me the time?" Bloodstone turns to asks Miss Sierra with boredom.

"Um . . . sure." Miss Sierra looks to her wristwatch. She repeats the time to Bloodstone with confusion. "It is 11:59 p.m., Mister Bloodstone."

"Almost midnight . . ." Bloodstone rubs his chin before returning to El Chupacabra, who is visibly vexed with the Masked Philanthropist's aloofness. "I've changed my mind Chupacabra. I shan't be killing you today, but I'll be taking my box with me now. The hour is late, and I've been up for days, so I'm in need of a good-night's rest."

"You . . . won't be killing me?" El Chupaca-bra's left eye twitches. He is greatly irate with

Bloodstone's blatant disrespect towards his authority.

"Oh, dear me. It seems I misspoke. My humblest apologies Chupacabra, truth be told, I had every intention to kill you once I've reclaimed my box. But the more I thought about it, the more I realized your demise wouldn't be in Cuckoo Meadows' best interest nor its people." Bloodstone reaches into his jacket and pulls out another cigar. He chomps on it and lights it with his silver Zippo lighter. He continues with streams of smoke jetting out from his flared nostrils. "You see, Chupacabra, your death will create nothing but a power vacuum, and then, quite predictably, war for your vacant throne will occur. And who's to say the next buffoon to covet for the crown of the criminal underground won't be as overzealous as you once were. I don't want to have to break another one in. I much prefer to keep the rabid dog already on leash."

"You dare mock me?!" El Chupacabra's eyes flare with blind fury. Veins crack the smooth dome of his scalp. He grabs the black box and waves it in front of Bloodstone's face, and barks: "People think you're some sort of a god sent to them from the heavens, but I will show them that even gods kneel before El Chupacabra. Heh-heh. Lookit that, I too, have had a change of heart, Bloodstone. Now, I will show them that even gods bleed."

El Chupacabra snaps his fingers and all five Tommy Guns cock with a fixed mark on Bloodstone and Miss Sierra.

"Mister Bloodstone, I'm sorry to say this to you right now, but I'm finding that my newfound faith in you might've been a tad premature." Miss Sierra leans her back up against Bloodstone's. This time around, she is uncertain the Masked Philanthropist will walk away unscathed. "Whatever you're planning to do, I suggest you do it now."

"Calm yourself, Miss Sierra. Now is not the time for either of us to soil our undergarments. Besides, this isn't the first time I've been in a tight bind. And if you will indulge me, I'll gladly share the tale with you right now." Bloodstone takes a drag from his cigar. All eyes fixate on him with childlike anticipation. He continues, uninterrupted. "Back in the early summer of '77, a young and talented Japanese mangaka by the name of Hirohiko Araki joined me in an adventure across the hot Mexican deserts. He sought out inspiration for the next chapter of his manga masterpiece, and I was in the pursuit of Nazi occultists who conspired to awaken an ancient Aztec mummy. And 'twas sheer misfortune which thrusted poor Araki into my mission to foil the Nazi's sinister plot of world conquest. Yet, nonetheless, he was a trooper to the end."

Bloodstone pauses for a moment to take another drag from his cigar. Miss Sierra is immediately impressed with the Masked Philanthropist's storytelling gifts. The goons, and even El Chupacabra, have unquestionably fallen under the spell of Bloodstone's Mexican odyssey.

He continues.

"After two weeks, the chase came to its natural climax. Araki and I arrived at the subterranean pyramid too late. By then, the Nazis had already resurrected the Aztec mummy. There we were, outnumbered, outgunned, and with the world on the verge of eternal damnation. All hope seemed lost until Araki suggested a secret maneuver that bordered between lunacy and brilliance. Only thanks to his quick thinking that we survived the ordeal and managed to save the world in the end."

"Um . . . that's a fantastic tale, Mister

Bloodstone. A story for the children to enjoy. Though I don't see the point of it right now." Miss Sierra said snippily.

"Then allow me to illuminate you, Miss Sierra. We shall execute Araki's secret maneuver." Bloodstone replies with a glint of mischief in his eyes.

"We are?" Miss Sierra asks.

"Yes," Bloodstone replies confidently.

"Pray tell, Mister Bloodstone, how will we go about it?" Miss Sierra asks. She notices El Chupacabra, and his goons are equally curious about this secret maneuver.

"We shall use our legs," Bloodstone pats his legs, "and execute it to our last breath."

"I'm . . . confused." Miss Sierra said with worry.

"Enough with the stalling, Bloodstone!" El Chupacabra howls. "What are you planning? I demand to know this instant!"

Bloodstone chuckles and jets out smoke from his nostrils again. Then in a flash, without warning, the Masked Philanthropist flicks the cigar stub to the side, dashes forward like a squall, and slugs El Chupacabra across the face. The piggish mobster is flung clear across the room, with an overarching stream of blood trailing behind, and he drops the black box mid-flight before crashing against the brick wall in a dust cloud. Bloodstone instinctively grabs the black box off the floor and bolts it. With legs and arms flailing up in the air, the Masked Philanthropist yells back to Miss Sierra: "Let's get the fuck out of here, Miss Si—iera!"

The Masked Philanthropist gets a few paces ahead before Miss Sierra or the five goons realize what has just happened. They exchange confused glances with one another. She chuckles nervously and utters a quick, "Oh, dear Lord," and runs after Bloodstone.

El Chupacabra jumps back up. He scowls his men with spewing blood. "Don't just stand there, you eunuch fucks! Rain lead down on them; I want their carcasses looking like Swiss Cheese!"

"Quickly, Miss Sierra, up the stairs!" Bloodstone orders once he knocks down the double doors clear off the hinges. A swarm of bullets follows shortly thereafter. "We need to get to the fifth floor."

They gallop three flights up, and once Miss Sierra catches her breath, she yells to Bloodstone: "This is most unorthodox, Mister Bloodstone! Did you not pluck bullets off the air back at Huan Wu's Gun Pow Chicken? And is your chest not speckled with bullets? Bullets, which I may add, remain buried deep in your chest. I'm weary of asking so many questions, but I have to know, given everything, why are we running?"

Midway up the fourth flight, Bloodstone finally answers her inquiries. "I must confess, Miss Sierra, Shen Yan was not mistaken when he suspected me incapable of plucking an entire barrage of bullets. We were most fortunate the rest of his brotherhood did not dare to test his theory. And, I had a pair of chopsticks then, which I lack right now. As for the pattern of bullets over my chest, well, answer me this first. Have you ever been shot before?"

"No, can't say I have." Miss Sierra said. A bullet suddenly whizzes past her right cheek. "And I'm in no rush to share the experience."

"Well—quickly down the corridor to the left." Bloodstone directs immediately after they set foot on the fifth level. He then continues, "I've been shot numerous times in the past, and I'm unashamed to admit every single time it really, really, really hurt."

A dead end. Bloodstone and Miss Sierra have reached the end of the corridor. There are no other stairs, doors, or even windows, only a brick wall. They have nowhere else to run.

"They made a left over here. We got them cornered boys. Hurry."—the goon named Pauly yells. Their trotting footsteps and the accompanying clink of their Tommy Guns close in fast.

"Seems pointless to try and resign now. And I do hope you understand if I hate you, don't you, Mister Bloodstone?" Miss Sierra said in resignation.

"Refresh my memory, Miss Sierra. You do know how to swim, correct?" Bloodstone asks.

"Yes . . . how is that of any relevance—?" Miss Sierra's breath is snatched, along with the rest of her body. She is pulled in tight against Bloodstone's chest.

The Masked Philanthropist cradles her between his muscular and broad arms. "Hold on tight, Miss Sierra,"—Bloodstone exclaims, seconds before he bulldozes through the brick wall with the full blunt force of his entire body. The entire wall explodes in a loud dust cloud of brick pebbles.

"Oh . . . my . . . Go—od!" Miss Sierra yells.

And they plummet onto the icy, ocean waves below.

CHAPTER 9

THE McGUFFIN

A mist of bubbles surrounds them on impact with the thrashing ocean waves. From above, zigging bullets pelt blindly with lead fury, and soon after, jets of red strings dissolve quickly as they materialize in the briny depths.

Alarmed, Miss Sierra gropes her entire body, thinking a bullet might have stung her but is too numb from the icy dive to notice. To her immediate relief, the blood isn't hers. A powerful grip locks around her shoulders, and her drowned yelps rob her of precious breaths. The hand cups her mouth and saves Miss Sierra from a quick, watery death.

The Masked Philanthropist still holds on to his prized box, and he guides Miss Sierra's gaze up to the surface with his eyes. Bloodstone's wagging finger hints to the obvious—to emerge above the surface while the goons' bullets still needle the waters is unsafe, and the bleeding gash on his right shoulder confirms this needlessly said fact. Miss Sierra shakes her head with alarm, motioning with her hands that she cannot hold her breath much longer.

A soft olive glow draws their attention slightly below their paddling feet, and Miss Sierra's joyful tears turn invisible underwater. The rippling rings are the same portal markings the Pulque Bunny, Anton, created earlier at the alley. Sheer survival instinct drives Miss Sierra toward the shimmering portal. Bloodstone follows shortly behind, and with a soft thud, both flop aboard the service boat's wooden deck—the same service boat that had been patrolling the coast.

Miss Sierra gasps for air. She frantically peeks through the white disks of light and recognizes the two figures beside her. The two Pulque Bunnies, Macario and Anton, are accompanied by a third individual she does not recognize.

He is a slim man, taller than Anton but shorter than Macario. A dirty red blazer swathes his body with the neck collar wrapping around the mouth. A black striped headband divides the slim man's forehead from the spiked hair and two-pronged antlers that sprout from his scalp like thorns. No introductions are needed. Miss Sierra deduces this third queer character is none other than the penitent Block.

"Hiya boss, cold night for a swim, yes?" Block said dryly.

"Your reliable dry humor is insufficient to quell my bitterness this time around, Block." Bloodstone snaps back angrily to Block, who lowers his head like a scorned child. But, in the end, the Masked Philanthropist's nobler side cools his fiery scorn. "Still, I'm more than happy to see you back home. I do not know how, old friend, but I will find a way to convince the old gargoyle to release you three from the pact you've been coerced into with him. For the time being, let us go home. The day has been long, and I'm more than a bit tired."

"Mister Bloodstone, look!" Miss Sierra shouts. She points to El Chupacabra from a distance. He waves a clenched fist to them from the gaping hole Bloodstone bulldozed through the wall. "He's yelling something to us. I can't tell what over the waves, and we're too far away from the harbor."

"I can only imagine. Most likely the usual

'you haven't seen the last of me, this isn't over'—
or something similar of the threatening sort.
That's the thing about egotistical mobsters,
Miss Sierra. They're so boringly predictable."
Bloodstone sets his black box down to the side
and picks up a stray metal nut. He squints his
eyes and measures the distance between them
and El Chupacabra. The Mask Philanthropist
then leisurely pulls back his arm like a sling
and then throws the metal nut with blunt
force. From afar, El Chupacabra is seen falling
back. Bloodstone hit the mark.

"Bullseye!"—he exclaims proudly.

"What did you do?" Miss Sierra asks
disapprovingly.

"Nothing too crude. I simply shattered his
front teeth. Gruel and broth and dietary milk-
shakes shall be his comfort meals for weeks
until the dentures come in, of course." Bloodstone said with a snicker.

⸻ ⸻

Miss Sierra retreats to her wristwatch in search
of some sort of comfort. She smiles weakly. It
still functions perfectly. The hour ticks thirty
minutes past midnight, and she sighs a small
laugh, unable to believe the bizarre adventure

she has just undergone. Cuckoo Meadows truly is a majestic gem. No longer will she view the world through myopic eyes for her world has broadened onto unimaginable, weirder frontiers. Her life is no longer confined to the written page's rigid borders, and perhaps, one day her own spun tall tales will, too, broaden the scope of another young girl's englobed existence. The more she thinks about it, the more she falls in love with the dream.

The little boat carelessly careens along Sugar Hill Pier's moon-kissed coastline. At the helm, Anton maneuvers the vessel towards the howling opening of a sewer outfall, and they enter Cuckoo Meadows' subterranean sewer tunnels. Macario hops towards the boat's bow and wiggles his short-pointy nose, eager to sniff the labyrinthine tunnels' many rancid smells. And for the remainder of their leisurely trip, the Masked Philanthropist is in deep conversation with Block at the stern. Miss Sierra keeps to herself and respects their privacy. Though, in all honesty, she has no desire to delve into any more bizarre matters. Old gargoyles, magickal pacts, and devil may care antics—things of weirder fiction best left alone for another time and future bizarre ventures.

When they finally come to a halt, the wristwatch read 1:00 a.m. on the dot. Bloodstone is the first to jump off the boat and, ever the gentleman, offers Miss Sierra a hand. Exhaustion wins her over, and she welcomes the kind gesture. The trio of Pulque Bunnies decides not to linger much longer and bid them a cheeky goodbye. They then wash away along with the rest of Cuckoo Meadows' sewage, immersed in a merry song.

Bloodstone taps a series of bricks in a mazelike pattern. Miss Sierra attempts to memorize it, but exhaustion hinders her thinking, and she simply gives up. A soft, stony grind follows, and a hidden elevator door is revealed. The Masked Philanthropist explains to Miss Sierra without invitation; around three years ago, he had his Pulque Bunnies install a secret passage that connects his skyward penthouse to Cuckoo Meadows' subterranean sewer tunnels. This secret elevator allows him to come and go as he pleases, to indulge his puckish habits free of the commitment to apprise those who cling to him and his shadow out of necessity rather than desire.

"I am a simple man, Miss Sierra. Though this megacorporation bears my name, I am not fully bound to it. Such a corporate sphere, bores me, quite painfully. And from time to time, I do crave an escape onto the throes of adventure." Bloodstone comments aloud during the elevator's slow rise towards his skyward penthouse.

A short melodic ping preludes the steel doors' opening. Miss Sierra's eyes touch upon a massive cornucopia of ancient artifacts, the likes of which she has never seen before.

They have arrived at the Masked Philanthropist's sacred vault.

Fossils of strange beasts, living monuments of unearthly nightmares, encase most of the wall cavities. Dozens of well-lit display cases house many ancient trinkets and strange artifacts. Each artifact is labeled with a bronze plaque inscribed with a brief annotation. But of all the artifacts, from the strangely inapposite battered battle ax with the acronym G.Y. over the grain of its haft to the human-sized skull of an owl and the golden-lined crystal flask containing the blood of Tlahuicole, none seduces her attention more than the horrific leather mask.

The mask conjures the memory of a similar hollow, stone face from her youth. It invokes the memory surrounding the death of her little brother, Santiago. But this thing is different—an organic monstrosity. The ashen *calavera* mask with frizzled charcoal-white hair exhumes terror from its bone-like hide, and the hollow orifices—those vacant, hateful eyes—near convince Miss Sierra that the demonic mask breathes and rapes the sanctity of her very soul. The plaque underneath it reads Ixpuxtequi, 1588–c.1985 and the inscription: "*El giro del destino es inevitable.*"

"*What an ugly thing, no doubt pinioned to a much uglier story*"—Miss Sierra thinks to herself.

"Miss Sierra, would you please join me over here." Bloodstone calls out to her.

"It's quite a beautiful collection you have here, Mister Bloodstone. Well, mostly." Miss Sierra said, looking back to the monstrous mask.

"And yet, I would trade it all for what's inside this little black box," Bloodstone replies. "You helped me reclaim that which is most precious to me and at great personal risk no less. It is only fair I show you what is inside this here, little black box. Would you like that, Miss Sierra?"

"I'd be deeply honored, Mister Bloodstone."

Miss Sierra's eyes light up with joy. After overcoming many death-defying feats, she will finally discover the nature of Bloodstone's most prized treasure. It is a fitting reward. Her mind skims through the pages of wonder absorbed in her youth with high expectations of the item's identity. Could it be the heart of a true Chupacabra? A golden calabash fruit from the sacred gardens of Xibalba? Or perhaps, the Masked Philanthropist's severed soul?

Bloodstone opens the polished black box and pulls out his most treasured item. To Miss Sierra's mild ire, Bloodstone's most precious treasure turns out to be nothing of paranormal intrigue nor supernatural wealth. This treasure which has aroused Bloodstone's wrath and vengeful spirit is nothing more than a run-of-the-mill plastic, brown horse.

"A horse? A plastic horse?" Miss Sierra scoffs with resentment. She gives off an irritable, half-hearted laugh. "This thing's what we risked our lives for? Mine more than yours. Oh, Lord. You truly are something special, Mister Blood-stone—a special type of weird. I'd call you crazy, but it's too sane of a word for you."

"An insignificant little toy, I agree, Miss Sierra. But only when seen through ignorant eyes." Bloodstone's compassionate spirit understands Miss Sierra's scornful attitude. He then allows his ripe, tired soul to speak to her with the hope that she may understand. "I've roved about the prairies of eternity for nigh three hundred years, Miss Sierra—an eternity of heroic feats. And yet, no matter the countless people and nations preserved, villains conquered, and stories spun, Death's torment remains unyielding. I've come to know the horror and hopelessness of hearing loved ones—their voices and names—forever fall silent, quite intimately. This here little horse, plastic and weightless as it may be, anchors heavy over my heart. Whenever I look to it, I am taken back to a more carefree time. Ofttimes, I can still smell the hot chocolate my *Mamá Sofia* brewed for me that one cold, rainy morning—it was my 8th birthday. Humble and poor, she spent what few pesos she had for her medication and bought me this very horse instead. Just to see me smile. This little horse is a constant reminder of the value of love and sacrifice. The world around me has irrevocably changed, Miss Sierra, and yet, this little horse still fetters me to a time I shall never relive, to people I shall never see again, not even in death."

Bloodstone's emotional confession humbles Miss Sierra. She finally understands the reason why he risked life and limb to reclaim such an invaluable treasure. Bloodstone covets something richer than material wealth or the masses' blind worship. He treasures the small, vaporous memories that ultimately shape us. Memories that are often carelessly overlooked and pined at the deathbed by mortal fools who chased after immortality. She avoids the Masked Philanthropist's tender gaze, ashamed for having scorned him so without first trying to understand.

"Mister Bloodstone." Miss Sierra said, twiddling her fingers. "I—I apologize. I didn't know."

"Worry not, Miss Sierra." Bloodstone chuckles. He then wipes off the thin veil of tears swelled over his eyes. "The eccentricities of an immortal are not easily tolerated. An odd thing to believe, is it not? Above all the other more flamboyant mementos accumulated through-out the centuries, it is this little horse that is the purest of treasures. Then again, there will never be no other person like my Mamá Sofia."

Miss Sierra recalls newscaster Robbie's comments about Bloodstone from the previous day and finally understands why the Masked Philanthropist elected her as his personal assistant. He wanted someone who would see past the titles inscribed to him—Bloodstone the C.E.O., Bloodstone the Philanthropist, Bloodstone the Storyteller—and past the myriad of other misrepresentations the people might have about him and see him for who he truly is, Bloodstone, the man. Mask or no mask, Miss Sierra will forever only see this man before her.

"By the way, Miss Sierra, I'd like to take this moment to formally welcome you to Bloodstone Enterprises," Bloodstone said with a warm smile. "As you have learned throughout this wondrous adventure, this will be no ordinary job."

Miss Sierra smiles, and her eyes glint with anticipation for their next adventure. After a short pause, she finally replies: "I wouldn't have it any other way, Mister Bloodstone."

www.ingramcontent.com/pod-product-compliance
Lightning Source LLC
Chambersburg PA
CBHW021141190726

48288CB00008B/2774